Reboot Sofa: The Wonderland Gamble

A Virtual Adventure of Love and Mystery

Emmanuel Simms

In Vivo Exposure Publishing

IN VIVO EXPOSURE
CONSULTING

CONTENTS

CHAPTER 1 - INTRODUCTION

The TV studio was a frenzied cacophony of noise and movement. The room was brightly lit, cameras glinting in the light.. Amid the chaos, a figure emerged, a woman of powerful character but somewhat uncertain demeanor. Her name was Alice.

Alice was a single mother of two, a literature teacher whose life revolved around her children and her classroom. She had a keen intellect and a boundless passion for literature, finding solace and inspiration within the pages of classic books. Alice's love for literature was not just an escape; it was her lifeline, her connection to the broader world.

As Alice navigated through the studio, she felt a surge of excitement. Her heart pounded with the thrill of this new adventure, of stepping so far outside her comfort zone. She had always been a private person, her quiet world centered on her classroom and her children. But this opportunity, appearing on the TV show "Reboot Sofa", was too intriguing to pass up.

Alice's eyes scanned the room, taking in the busy crew members, the expensive equipment, and the flashy stage set. It was a far cry from her cozy classroom filled with well-thumbed books and eager young minds. She was in a different world now, a world that was as exciting as it was intimidating.

Meanwhile, a tall, imposing man stepped into the studio. His name was Sherlock, a criminology professor at a renowned university. He was a man of few words but exceptional intellect, known for his knack for puzzles and his unyielding passion for his field. Sherlock was a widower, the world of crime and mystery offering a strange comfort in the solitude of his grief.

He observed the surrounding commotion with a stoic expression, his keen eyes flicking around the room, assessing, and analyzing. His university life was ordered and predictable, but the chaotic environment offered something different that he wanted to experience..

Sherlock's eyes settled on Alice from across the room, and he felt an immediate spark of curiosity. There was something about her, a mix of strength and vulnerability that intrigued him. He found himself wondering what her story was, what had brought her to the "Reboot Sofa."

At the same moment, Alice turned and her gaze met Sherlock's. Her heart fluttered in her chest. She could tell, just from that brief moment of eye contact, that he was a man of great intellect. She found herself drawn to him, his aura of mystery, his calm demeanor amidst the chaos.

As Alice and Sherlock were introduced on stage by the show's vivacious host, Emily, a sense of anticipation filled the air. Both of them felt it, a tantalizing potential for something special, something that could change their lives forever.

As the lights of the studio dimmed, the audience quietened, and Emily, the host, began her introduction. Alice and Sherlock found themselves seated side by side on the plush, inviting sofa, the mainstay of the "Reboot Sofa" show. They exchanged an awkward but curious glance, the electricity between them almost tangible.

Emily started off the conversation with some light-hearted banter, her effervescent personality cutting through the initial tension. Both Alice and Sherlock found themselves warming up to her and the audience. They shared their personal stories, their passion for literature and mysteries, their life as educators, and the solitary journey of parenting.

Their conversation meandered from discussing their favorite books to recounting the challenges and rewards of parenthood, interspersed with Emily's engaging questions and comments. The atmosphere gradually relaxed, and an easy camaraderie developed among them. Alice found herself laughing at Sherlock's dry humor, while Sherlock admired Alice's insightful comments and her infectious enthusiasm for literature.

By the end of the recording, the initial nerves had faded away, replaced by a sense of accomplishment and the beginnings of a unique bond. They parted ways with a promise to meet again for the next episode, both aware that their journey on the "Reboot Sofa" was just beginning.

Later that night, both Alice and Sherlock found themselves in the quiet confines of their homes, replaying the day's events. Alice, ensconced in her cozy reading nook, mulled over the intriguing man she had met. Sherlock, with his profound intellect and dry humor, was unlike any man she had met before. Despite his slightly aloof demeanor, she sensed a depth to him that intrigued her.

Simultaneously, Sherlock found himself in his study, surrounded by a mess of papers and case files, but his thoughts were far from work. He found himself thinking about Alice, her passionate discussion about literature, and the way her eyes sparkled when she talked about her favorite books. She was different, he realized, from the people he usually interacted with.

A quiet sense of anticipation lingered in the air as they both found themselves looking forward to their next meeting. Little did they know, their lives were about to take a turn they never anticipated. As the night fell and they retreated into their respective worlds, the promise of tomorrow hung in the air – filled with the potential of new friendships and unexpected discoveries.

With the stage set and their lives unknowingly intertwined, Alice and Sherlock had embarked on a journey that promised more than they could've imagined. The Reboot Sofa was no longer just a reality show; it was the start of something that was going to reboot their lives in ways they had never envisioned.

CHAPTER 2: UNEXPECTED CHALLENGES

The TV studio was a whirlwind of activity as Alice stepped into the bustling room, her heart racing with anticipation. She scanned the area, searching for a glimpse of the man who had ignited her curiosity—Sherlock, the enigmatic criminology professor. And then she saw him, standing tall and composed amidst the chaos.

Their eyes locked, and the air crackled with an undeniable electricity. Sherlock made his way towards her, a ghost of a smile playing on his lips.

"Hello, Alice," Sherlock said, his voice low and velvety.

"Hi, Sherlock," she replied, her breath catching in her throat. "It's finally nice to meet you in person."

Sherlock's gaze lingered on her, his eyes filled with an intensity that sent a shiver down her spine. "Likewise, Alice. I must admit, our previous conversations have left me intrigued."

A blush crept up Alice's cheeks as she averted her gaze. "You have that effect on me too. There's something about your mind, your words... They captivate me."

Sherlock chuckled softly, the sound like music to her ears. "I'm glad to know I have an effect on you, Alice. You've piqued my curiosity from the moment we started talking."

As Emily, the charismatic host, approached them, Alice's attention was torn away from Sherlock. Emily's voice was filled with excitement as she introduced them, her eyes gleaming with anticipation.

"Alice, meet Sherlock," Emily said, her voice bubbling with enthusiasm. "And Sherlock, this is Alice. You two are going to make an incredible pair on the show."

Alice glanced back at Sherlock, a mix of nerves and excitement bubbling within her. "I can't wait to dive into the world of literature with you, Sherlock. I have a feeling it's going to be an unforgettable experience."

Sherlock's gaze never wavered as he nodded, a hint of a smile playing on his lips. "I share the same sentiment, Alice. I believe our connection runs deeper than our shared love for books."

As they settled onto the plush sofa, the room seemed to fade away, leaving just the two of them in their own world. The cameras started rolling, capturing every moment of their first meeting.

Emily, the host, directed their attention to the first question, and the conversation flowed effortlessly. Their words danced between them, each revelation deepening their connection.

Alice couldn't help but be drawn to Sherlock's piercing gaze, his intellect shining through every word he spoke. She found herself hanging onto his every sentence, craving to unravel the layers of mystery that surrounded him.

Sherlock, too, was captivated by Alice's warmth and passion, her ability to bring stories to life and make the written word dance off the page. He was entranced by the way her eyes sparkled when she spoke about her favorite books and the way her laughter filled the room.

Time seemed to slip away as they delved into their personal stories, sharing glimpses of their pasts, their dreams, and their fears. With each revelation, their connection deepened, like two souls finding solace in the shared understanding of their vulnerabilities.

As the cameras stopped rolling and the chapter came to a close, Alice and Sherlock shared a moment of quiet intimacy. Their eyes locked once again, the world around them fading into the background.

"Thank you for this incredible conversation, Alice," Sherlock said softly, his voice filled with sincerity. "It's rare to find someone who truly understands the power of literature and its ability to shape our lives."

Alice's heart swelled with emotion as she reached out, her hand gently touching Sherlock's. "And thank you, Sherlock, for sharing a part of yourself with me. There's so much more I want to discover about you."

They both knew that their journey had just begun, that their connection held the promise of something extraordinary. As they parted ways, a single thought lingered in their minds—a thought that would propel them forward, eager to explore the depths of their shared passion and the depths of their hearts.

Alice and Sherlock found themselves drawn to each other, unable to resist the magnetic pull between them. They stole glances, exchanged knowing smiles, and engaged in playful banter throughout the rest of the filming session.

As the day wore on, the initial nerves gave way to a growing comfort and familiarity. They discovered shared interests beyond literature—music, art, and even their favorite coffee shops. Their conversations flowed effortlessly, the words forming a beautiful symphony between them.

During a break, as they found a moment of privacy away from the prying eyes of the crew, Sherlock leaned in closer to Alice, his voice laced with a hint of vulnerability. "Alice, there's something about you that captivates me. Your passion, your intellect... I can't deny the connection between us."

Alice's heart skipped a beat, her breath catching in her throat. She gazed into Sherlock's eyes, her own filled with a mixture of anticipation and hesitancy. "Sherlock, I feel it too. There's a depth to you that calls to me, a yearning to unravel the enigma that lies within. But we must tread carefully. Our lives are complicated, and the path to love is not always smooth."

Sherlock nodded, understanding the weight of Alice's words. "You're right, Alice. We both carry our own baggage, our own fears and responsibilities. But perhaps, in each other, we can find the strength and support we need to navigate the complexities of life."

Their unspoken understanding hung in the air, the uncharted territory of their burgeoning connection stretching out before them. It was both exhilarating and terrifying, the possibility of love intertwined with the risks of heartache and uncertainty.

As the filming for the day concluded, Alice and Sherlock found themselves walking side by side, the hum of excitement still buzzing within them. The sun began to set, casting a golden glow over their surroundings, as if to mirror the warmth that blossomed within their hearts.

Alice turned to Sherlock, her voice filled with a newfound determination. "Sherlock, I don't know where this journey will lead us, but I'm willing to take a chance. Life is too short to ignore the spark we feel. Let's explore what lies between us, embracing the unknown with open hearts."

Sherlock's gaze softened, his lips curling into a genuine smile. "Alice, I couldn't agree more. Together, let's venture into uncharted territory, discovering the depths of our connection and the possibilities that lie ahead."

As they reached the exit of the studio, Alice and Sherlock shared a lingering gaze, the unspoken promise of their shared journey hanging in the air. They knew that their lives were about to change, that love had found a way into their hearts, and that the road ahead would be both challenging and rewarding.

With renewed hope and a sense of anticipation, they bid each other farewell, their hearts brimming with excitement for the next chapter of their story.

CHAPTER 3: LEARNING ABOUT EACH OTHER

Alice and Sherlock, both still buzzing with the excitement of their connection, decide to meet outside of the show's set. They find a cozy café, tucked away from the bustling city streets, where they can have a private conversation and learn more about each other beyond the cameras.

As they step into the café, the aroma of freshly brewed coffee fills the air, creating an atmosphere of warmth and intimacy. They find a corner table, nestled beside a large window that offers a view of the bustling city outside.

Alice, her eyes bright with anticipation, takes a seat opposite Sherlock. She can't help but notice the way his eyes sparkle with a mixture of curiosity and intrigue. This moment feels surreal to her, as if they've stepped into a world where only their presence matters.

Sherlock, ever observant, takes in the surroundings. The soft lighting casts a warm glow on the walls adorned with artwork, creating an ambiance of comfort and relaxation. The low hum of conversation and the clinking of coffee cups provide a soothing soundtrack to their meeting.

They order their drinks—a fragrant latte for Alice and a strong black coffee for Sherlock—and settle into their chairs. The air between them crackles with anticipation, their eyes locked in a dance of curiosity.

As they lean in closer, their conversation begins. The noise of the café fades into the background as they immerse themselves in each other's stories, eager to uncover the layers that make them who they are.

In this intimate setting, away from the scrutiny of the cameras, Alice and Sherlock have a chance to reveal their true selves. They peel back the layers, sharing their hopes, dreams, and the challenges they've overcome. They speak with a vulnerability that deepens their connection and strengthens the bond forming between them.

As the conversation unfolds, they find solace in each other's presence, a safe space where they can be their authentic selves without judgment or pretense. The café becomes a cocoon, shielding them from the outside world, allowing them to dive into the depths of their experiences and emotions.

It is in this moment, amidst the scent of coffee and the shared vulnerability, that Alice and Sherlock begin to understand each other on a deeper level. The barriers between them slowly dissolve, replaced by a sense of trust and mutual understanding.

Their journey of learning about each other has only just begun, but in this café, surrounded by the aroma of freshly brewed coffee and the warmth of their connection, Alice and Sherlock know that something extraordinary is unfolding—a love story that goes beyond the boundaries of reality television.

Alice takes a deep breath, gathering her thoughts as she begins to share her story. She opens up about the joys and struggles of being a single mother, the delicate balance she has had to strike between her responsibilities at home and her passion for literature.

With a touch of nostalgia in her voice, she talks about her journey as a young woman who fell in love with the written word. She shares how her mother, an avid reader herself, instilled in her a love for literature from a young age. Books became her refuge, her companions through the highs and lows of life.

Alice's voice softens as she speaks about the loss of her husband, a wound that still feels raw at times. She recounts the devastating impact it had on her and her children, the long nights spent searching for solace within the pages of her favorite novels. She shares how grief reshaped her outlook on life, making her appreciate the fleeting nature of love and the importance of cherishing every moment.

As she delves deeper, Alice discusses the challenges she faced in raising her children while navigating the complexities of being a single mother. She talks about the late nights spent grading papers, the sacrifices made to ensure her children had a stable and nurturing environment, and the endless juggling act of work, parenting, and personal growth.

But amidst the challenges, Alice's eyes light up as she talks about the moments of joy and fulfillment that come with being a mother and a teacher. She shares heartwarming anecdotes about her children's milestones and the impact she has made on her students' lives through her passion for literature. Her voice brims with pride and gratitude as she speaks about the incredible connections she has formed with her students, knowing that she has played a small part in shaping their futures.

As Alice finishes recounting her journey, there's a sense of resilience and determination in her voice. Despite the hardships she has faced, she radiates a quiet strength and a belief in the transformative power of love and literature. She looks at Sherlock, her eyes shimmering with a mix of vulnerability and hope, eager to hear his story, to understand the depths of his experiences and the reasons that led him to the present moment.

Sherlock takes a moment to gather his thoughts, his gaze fixed on a distant point as he prepares to open up about his own journey. He begins by recounting the tragedy that changed the course of his life, the loss of his beloved wife. The weight of his words is evident as he speaks of the void her absence left behind and the challenges he faced in single-handedly raising their son.

With a tinge of sadness in his voice, Sherlock shares how he sought solace in his work as a criminology professor, delving into the minds of criminals, and unraveling the intricate web of mysteries. He describes the emotional toll that his profession can sometimes take, the weight of darkness he carries as he unravels the secrets hidden within crime scenes and investigates the darkest corners of human behavior.

Sherlock's voice takes on a more animated tone as he recounts his early fascination with criminology, tracing it back to his childhood. He shares stories of how he would spend hours engrossed in detective novels, eagerly trying to solve the puzzles and outsmart the villains alongside his literary heroes. It was during those formative years that his passion for the intricacies of crime and the pursuit of justice took root.

As he speaks, Sherlock's eyes glimmer with a mixture of intensity and vulnerability, revealing the emotional connection he has forged with his work. He explains how his journey into criminology became a coping mechanism, a way to channel his grief and find purpose in unraveling mysteries. It became a lifeline, a refuge that provided him with a sense of control in a world that felt chaotic and unpredictable.

Sherlock's narrative concludes with a note of gratitude for the unwavering support of his son, who became his anchor in the storm of grief. He expresses how his experiences have shaped him into the person he is today, instilling in him a profound appreciation for the fragility of life and the resilience of the human spirit.

As Alice listens intently to Sherlock's narrative, a sense of empathy and understanding fills her heart. She sees the pain and the strength intertwined in his words, recognizing a kindred spirit who has also weathered the storm of loss and emerged with a fierce determination to make a difference in the world.

With a soft smile, Alice reaches across the table, her fingers gently touching Sherlock's hand. "Sherlock, I can't express how much I admire your resilience and your dedication to your son. It's clear that family means everything to you, just as it does to me. We both understand the sacrifices and the joys that come with being a single parent, and I truly believe that it has shaped us into the people we are today."

Sherlock's eyes meet Alice's, a flicker of understanding passing between them. "Alice, you're right. The bond between a parent and their child is a powerful force that drives us to be the best version of ourselves. It's a responsibility that we both hold close to our hearts."

Their conversation deepens as they explore their shared values, realizing that they both value authenticity and genuine connections in a world that often feels superficial and disconnected. They discuss their passions for their respective fields, literature, and criminology, and how they strive to make a positive impact through their work.

"There's something incredibly rewarding about helping young minds discover the power of literature," Alice muses. "It's not just about the words on the page; it's about connecting with others, understanding different perspectives, and fostering empathy. I believe that literature has the power to change lives."

Sherlock nods in agreement, his eyes lighting up with enthusiasm. "And criminology, in its essence, is about seeking justice, unraveling the truth, and understanding the complexities of human behavior. It's about making a difference and creating a safer world for future generations."

In that moment, Alice and Sherlock realize that they share a profound desire to leave their mark on the world, to make a difference in the lives of others through their respective passions. Their connection deepens as they recognize the aligned values that underpin their individual journeys, creating a strong foundation upon which their relationship can grow.

As their conversation flows, Alice and Sherlock gradually peel back the layers of their vulnerability, sharing their deepest fears and insecurities. In this safe space they have created, they find solace and understanding, knowing that they can confide in each other without judgment.

Alice takes a deep breath, her gaze fixed on the table as she opens up about her own struggles. "Sherlock, being a single mother is both rewarding and challenging. There are moments when I doubt myself, when I worry if I'm doing enough for my children. Balancing my career as a teacher and being there for them is a constant juggling act. Sometimes, I fear that I'm not giving them the stability they need."

Sherlock reaches out, his hand gently covering Alice's, a comforting gesture that conveys his support. "Alice, I understand the weight of those fears. As a widower, I often question if I'm enough for my son. I worry about providing him with the guidance and love he deserves. There are times when I feel overwhelmed by the responsibilities on my shoulders."

Alice's eyes meet Sherlock's, their vulnerability creating an unspoken bond between them. "It's comforting to know that we're not alone in these struggles. And perhaps, together, we can navigate the challenges that come our way. We can be a source of strength and support for each other, reminding ourselves that it's okay to have doubts and fears."

Sherlock nods, his voice filled with reassurance. "Alice, you are an incredible mother, and I have no doubt that you're doing a phenomenal job. Your children are lucky to have you. And as for me, I'm learning that it's okay to ask for help and lean on those who care about me."

In that moment, a sense of understanding washes over them, as if a weight has been lifted. They find solace in each other's vulnerability, knowing that they can lean on one another during times of uncertainty. Together, they create a safe space where fears can be shared, and support can be offered unconditionally.

As Alice and Sherlock continue to share their stories, they stumble upon unexpected connections and coincidences that weave their lives together in ways they never imagined. It's as if the universe has been silently orchestrating their paths, leading them to this moment of profound connection.

Alice's eyes widen in astonishment as Sherlock mentions a small bookstore he used to frequent during his college years. "Wait, did you say 'Book Haven'? I used to work there part-time while I was studying literature! It was my sanctuary, a place where I found solace and lost myself in the pages of countless books."

Sherlock's face lights up with recognition, a smile tugging at the corners of his lips. "Book Haven? That's where I first discovered my love for crime novels! I remember a young woman with a passion for literature, always recommending the most intriguing titles. I never knew it was you."

They share a moment of wonder, realizing that their paths had crossed before, even if they were unaware of it at the time. It feels as if fate has been nudging them closer, leaving breadcrumbs for them to follow until they finally found themselves in this shared space of understanding and connection.

Alice reaches across the table, her hand finding Sherlock's, their fingers intertwining naturally. "It's incredible, isn't it? How life can bring us full circle, leading us back to the people who were meant to be a part of our journey. I believe there's a reason we're sitting here, discovering these connections."

Sherlock gazes into Alice's eyes, a mix of awe and gratitude in his expression. "I couldn't agree more, Alice. It's as if the universe has conspired to bring us together, to show us that our connection runs deeper than we ever imagined. I feel incredibly fortunate to have found you."

In that moment, the weight of the past and the uncertainties of the future fade into the background. Alice and Sherlock revel in the serendipity of their connection, knowing that they are meant to embark on this journey together, discovering the intricacies of their shared past and building a future that holds endless possibilities.

As their conversation unfolds, Alice and Sherlock become increasingly aware of the deepening attraction that simmers beneath the surface. It's not just their shared values and intellectual connection—it's something more profound, a magnetic pull that defies rational explanation.

Alice finds herself captivated by Sherlock's keen intellect, his ability to dissect complex ideas with ease. But it's his genuine kindness and the way he listens intently, as if her words hold immeasurable value, that truly tugs at her heart. There's a certain vulnerability in his eyes, a hint of longing that mirrors her own.

Sherlock, too, feels the intensity of the attraction. He admires Alice's strength and resilience, how she effortlessly balances her role as a mother and a teacher. But it's the spark in her eyes when she speaks about literature, the way her face lights up with passion, that stirs something deep within him. He's drawn to her magnetic energy, her curiosity, and the unspoken understanding that passes between them.

Their conversation takes on a new level of intimacy as they lean closer, their voices hushed as if sharing a secret. The air crackles with anticipation, their words laced with unspoken desires. They find themselves lingering on the edge of what could be, their hearts beating in synchrony.

Alice's fingers instinctively brush against Sherlock's hand, a fleeting touch that sends a jolt of electricity through both of them. Their eyes meet, and time seems to stand still for a brief moment. In that instant, the weight of unspoken words hangs heavily in the air, the uncharted territory of their burgeoning connection stretching out before them.

They exchange a knowing smile, a silent acknowledgment of the magnetic pull between them. It's a dance of temptation and restraint, a delicate balance of desires and the fear of risking their hearts once more. But in that shared gaze, they find solace and the courage to explore the uncharted depths of their attraction.

As the conversation between Alice and Sherlock reaches its peak, a sudden interruption breaks the spell. The show's producer approaches them with a mischievous grin, holding an envelope in his hand.

"Congratulations, Alice and Sherlock," he says, his voice filled with anticipation. "You've earned yourselves a spot in the next challenge. Brace yourselves for what's to come."

Alice and Sherlock exchange a curious glance, their hearts pounding with a mix of excitement and trepidation. The challenge looms ahead, a test that will push their newfound connection to its limits. They're left wondering what lies in store for them, how this challenge will shape their relationship and the path they've chosen.

As they bid each other farewell, their minds buzz with questions and possibilities. Will they rise to the challenge and emerge stronger than ever? Or will the pressure of the show and their own insecurities create insurmountable obstacles?

CHAPTER 4: THE REBOOT CHALLENGE

Set the scene of the upcoming challenge, taking place in a picturesque outdoor location. Alice and Sherlock arrive, their hearts fluttering with a mix of anticipation and nerves. They are greeted by the show's host, Emily, who reveals the details of the challenge.

The crisp morning air carried a sense of excitement as Alice and Sherlock made their way to the designated challenge location. Nestled in the heart of a lush forest, the setting was straight out of a fairytale. The soft rays of sunlight filtered through the trees, casting a warm golden glow on everything it touched.

Alice couldn't help but feel a surge of adrenaline coursing through her veins. This challenge was going to be different, more physically demanding than anything they had faced before. Her eyes met Sherlock's, and she could see a mix of determination and nerves reflected in his gaze. They were in this together.

As they approached the clearing, Emily, the show's vibrant host, appeared, her enthusiasm contagious. She welcomed them with a wide smile, her eyes sparkling with anticipation. "Welcome, Alice and Sherlock, to the

Reboot Challenge! Today, you'll be tested not only on your intellect but also on your physical prowess. Get ready for an adventure that will push you to your limits!"

Emily went on to explain the details of the challenge —an intricate series of obstacles designed to test their teamwork, problem-solving skills, and physical endurance. Alice listened intently, her mind racing with thoughts of how they would conquer each hurdle, determined to prove their mettle.

The challenge course stretched before them, a maze of ropes, walls, and puzzles, each obstacle demanding focus, strength, and quick thinking. Alice and Sherlock exchanged a glance, a silent pledge to support each other through every twist and turn.

With their hearts pounding and adrenaline coursing through their veins, Alice and Sherlock took their positions at the starting line. The countdown began, and they sprang into action, ready to face the Reboot Challenge head-on.

Emily explains the rules and objectives of the challenge. It involves a series of physical and mental tasks that will test their teamwork, trust, and problem-solving skills. Alice and Sherlock listen intently, exchanging glances as they mentally prepare themselves for the daunting task ahead.

Emily took a deep breath, her voice filled with excitement as she revealed the details of the Reboot Challenge. "Alice and Sherlock, today's challenge will push you to your limits, both physically and mentally. It's a test of teamwork, trust, and problem-solving skills."

She went on to explain that the challenge would consist of a series of tasks, each one designed to challenge their abilities and push them to work together. From scaling towering walls to deciphering intricate puzzles, they would need to rely on their strengths and communicate effectively to succeed.

Alice's heart raced as she absorbed the information. This was unlike anything she had ever done before, and the magnitude of the challenge was not lost on her. She glanced at Sherlock, and their eyes met, silently conveying their determination to conquer whatever lay ahead.

Sherlock's analytical mind was already at work, strategizing how they could navigate each task efficiently. He knew that their success would depend on their ability to communicate and trust each other's instincts. A sense of excitement coursed through his veins as he prepared himself mentally for the challenge.

Emily continued to outline the specific objectives of each task, providing them with a rough roadmap of what to expect. The challenges ranged from physical feats that required strength and agility to mental puzzles that demanded quick thinking and problem-solving skills.

As Emily finished her explanation, she locked eyes with Alice and Sherlock, her gaze filled with unwavering belief in their abilities. "Remember, the true test lies not only in your individual skills but in your ability to work as a team. Trust each other, communicate, and give it your all. The Reboot Challenge begins now!"

Alice and Sherlock exchanged a determined glance, a silent affirmation of their commitment to face this challenge together. They took a deep breath, steeling themselves for what lay ahead, ready to push their limits and prove the strength of their connection.

Alice and Sherlock realize that they must rely on each other to succeed in the challenge. They acknowledge the importance of trust, communication, and cooperation in order to overcome the obstacles they will face. Their bond strengthens as they discuss strategies and share their strengths and weaknesses.

With the challenge details laid out before them, Alice and Sherlock found themselves facing the undeniable truth: they would need to work as a team to conquer the upcoming tasks. It was a pivotal moment that required them to trust in each other's abilities and forge a strong bond of cooperation.

They sought a quiet spot away from the buzz of anticipation, their minds focused on the challenge that lay ahead. Sitting side by side, Alice and Sherlock discussed their individual strengths and weaknesses, recognizing that their unique skills could complement each other.

Alice, known for her quick thinking and ability to see connections others might miss, offered her insights. "Sherlock, your analytical mind is invaluable in deciphering complex puzzles. We can rely on your ability to see patterns and uncover hidden clues. Together, we can navigate this challenge with precision."

Sherlock nodded, acknowledging Alice's observations. "And

your intuition, Alice, your ability to sense underlying emotions and motivations, will be crucial in understanding the nuances of each task. We must trust our instincts and communicate openly to ensure we're always on the same page."

As they shared their strategies and exchanged ideas, their connection deepened. They recognized the power of their combined strengths, understanding that their individual talents were enhanced when united. Their conversations were filled with laughter, laced with excitement and anticipation for what they could achieve together.

In that moment, Alice and Sherlock made a pact: to support each other, to communicate honestly, and to embrace the challenges that lay ahead. They knew that the road would not be easy, but their trust in each other bolstered their confidence.

With their plan in place, they rose from their seats, ready to face the Reboot Challenge head-on. Their hearts beat in sync as they took each other's hands, a symbol of their commitment to this shared journey.

As they walked toward the challenge course, the world around them faded into the background. Their focus was on the task at hand, the obstacles that awaited them, and the unwavering trust they had in each other. Together, they were ready to conquer anything that came their way.

The challenge begins, and Alice and Sherlock dive into the first task. They encounter unexpected obstacles and setbacks, but their determination and combined intellect help them navigate through. They find themselves relying on their individual strengths and supporting each other through moments of difficulty.

As the challenge commenced, Alice and Sherlock found themselves immersed in a whirlwind of physical and mental obstacles. The first task was a test of agility and problem-solving, requiring them to navigate a complex maze while deciphering clues along the way.

Alice led the way, her mind sharp and focused as she analyzed the intricate patterns and signs. "Sherlock, I see a pattern emerging here. We need to follow the symbols in the order they appear, and it will lead us to the next checkpoint."

Sherlock nodded, his keen observation skills at play. "Indeed, Alice. Your quick thinking and attention to detail are remarkable. Let's stay in sync and move swiftly."

Their communication flowed seamlessly as they maneuvered through the maze, encountering unexpected twists and turns. At times, they faced dead ends and moments of doubt, but their unwavering trust in each other spurred them on.

Alice reached out a hand, offering support when Sherlock faced a particularly challenging climb. "You've got this, Sherlock. I know you're strong enough to overcome this obstacle. Believe in yourself."

Sherlock gripped her hand, his eyes meeting hers with gratitude. "Thank you, Alice. Your belief in me gives me strength. Together, we can conquer anything."

With renewed determination, they forged ahead, their shared resolve propelling them forward. Each hurdle they faced only served to deepen their connection, solidifying their bond.

In the end, they emerged triumphant from the first task, the taste of victory mingling with the sweat on their brows. Their synchronized breaths matched the rhythm of their beating hearts, a testament to their resilience and the power of their partnership.

As they caught their breath, Alice and Sherlock shared a moment of celebration, their smiles mirroring the elation in their souls. They knew that this challenge was just the beginning, that there would be more obstacles to overcome. But with their unwavering trust and shared determination, they were ready to face whatever came their way.

As the challenge progresses, Alice and Sherlock face moments of frustration and exhaustion. They provide emotional support and encouragement to each other, reminding themselves of the reasons they embarked on this journey. Their connection deepens as they witness each other's vulnerability and resilience.

In the heat of the challenge, Alice and Sherlock found themselves facing one obstacle after another. The physical exertion and mental strain began to take its toll, their bodies and minds yearning for respite.

Alice stumbled, her legs feeling heavy and her breathing labored. Sherlock, quick to react, caught her arm, concern etched on his face. "Alice, take a moment. Breathe. You're doing amazing, and I believe in you."

Alice's chest heaved as she took deep breaths, allowing

Sherlock's words to wash over her. She looked into his eyes, gratitude and determination shining through. "Thank you, Sherlock. Your belief in me means more than you know. Let's do this together."

With renewed determination, they pressed on, offering words of encouragement and support at every turn. They became each other's pillars of strength, providing solace and motivation when the going got tough.

Sherlock faced a particularly challenging mental puzzle, frustration evident on his face. Alice, seeing his struggle, stepped closer and rested a hand on his shoulder. "Sherlock, I know you have the solution within you. Trust your instincts, and let your brilliant mind guide you."

Sherlock's gaze locked with hers, gratitude and a flicker of determination shining in his eyes. "Alice, your unwavering belief in me fuels my resolve. I won't let us down."

Together, they tackled the hurdles with renewed vigor, their connection growing stronger with every step forward. They witnessed each other's vulnerability and resilience, finding solace in the shared understanding of the challenges they faced.

As the challenge neared its end, Alice and Sherlock found themselves standing on the precipice of victory. The emotional support they provided each other became a testament to their unwavering bond, proving that they were not just partners in the challenge, but partners in life.

After intense moments of perseverance, Alice and Sherlock successfully complete the final task of the challenge. Their victory fills them with a sense of accomplishment and joy. They share a celebratory moment, basking in the pride of their teamwork and the strength of their bond.

As the last obstacle is overcome, a wave of triumph washes over Alice and Sherlock. Their faces light up with exhilaration, their breaths coming in exhilarated gasps. They stand side by side, their hands tightly clasped, their eyes shining with a shared sense of achievement.

Alice can't help but let out a joyous laugh, the sound echoing through the air. "Sherlock, we did it! We conquered every hurdle, every setback. We make a formidable team."

Sherlock's eyes sparkle with pride, a rare smile gracing his lips. "Indeed, Alice. Our combined intellect and unwavering support have propelled us to this moment of triumph. I couldn't have asked for a better partner."

As their gazes lock, a surge of emotion passes between them, unspoken words hanging in the air. They have come so far in their journey, both individually and together. The challenge has not only tested their physical and mental strength but also fortified the bond that continues to grow between them.

In the midst of their victory, they find themselves enveloped in a wave of pure elation. They throw their arms around each other, celebrating their success with a tight embrace. The world around them fades into the background as they revel in the moment, the adrenaline still coursing through their veins.

Amid the cheers and applause from the crew, Alice pulls

back slightly, her eyes meeting Sherlock's. "Sherlock, I couldn't have asked for a more incredible partner. Thank you for pushing me, believing in me, and being by my side throughout this challenge."

Sherlock's voice is filled with sincerity as he replies, "Alice, you have amazed me with your resilience and unwavering spirit. You bring out the best in me, and I'm grateful for the opportunity to share this journey with you."

In that moment, their connection deepens further. They have conquered the challenge together, emerging not only as partners on the show but also as two souls intertwined in a journey of love and discovery.

As the sun begins to set, casting a warm glow over their celebration, Alice and Sherlock take a moment to savor the sweetness of their triumph. It is a milestone on their path, a testament to the strength of their bond, and a promise of more adventures to come.

In the aftermath of the challenge, Alice and Sherlock take a moment to catch their breath and reflect on their journey. They open up further, revealing hidden truths and vulnerabilities that deepen their connection. Secrets are unveiled, creating a stronger bond of trust between them.

As the exhilaration of their triumph begins to subside, Alice and Sherlock find themselves seeking solace in each other's presence. They retreat to a quiet spot away from the jubilant crowd, their eyes still shimmering with the echoes of their shared victory.

With a gentle sigh, Alice breaks the silence, her voice

carrying a mix of awe and vulnerability. "Sherlock, I never expected this journey to bring me so much more than just a chance to be on a TV show. It's as if every step we take together unravels something deeper within us."

Sherlock nods, his expression one of understanding. "Indeed, Alice. This experience has unearthed emotions I thought were buried deep within me. It's as if our connection has opened doors to parts of myself I had long forgotten."

The air hangs heavy with anticipation as they exchange glances, a newfound sense of trust radiating between them. They find themselves willing to share the secrets that have shaped them, to peel back the layers and reveal the vulnerable parts of their souls.

Alice takes a deep breath, summoning the courage to speak her truth. "Sherlock, there's something I haven't told anyone before. After my husband's passing, I closed myself off from the possibility of love. I was afraid of being hurt again, afraid of exposing my children to another loss. But being with you, Sherlock, it's like a ray of sunlight breaking through the darkness. You make me believe in the power of love once more."

Sherlock's eyes soften, his heart swelling with compassion. "Alice, I understand the fear of losing someone you hold dear. After my wife's tragic accident, I questioned if I could ever love again. But your presence in my life has shown me that love has the power to heal, to bring light to even the darkest corners of our hearts."

In that intimate moment, Alice and Sherlock find solace in

their shared vulnerability. They have unlocked the doors to their hearts, trusting each other with their deepest fears and desires. This unveiling of secrets creates a bond that transcends the boundaries of the show and paves the way for a profound connection.

As the sun begins to set, casting a warm, golden glow over their surroundings, Alice and Sherlock share a lingering embrace. They pull back, their eyes locked in a silent understanding.

"Sherlock," Alice whispers, her voice filled with a newfound confidence, "this journey we're on is just the beginning. I want to explore what lies between us, to see where this connection leads."

Sherlock smiles, his hand reaching out to gently caress Alice's cheek. "Alice, I couldn't agree more. Let's continue this adventure, stepping into the unknown hand in hand. I promise to cherish every moment with you, to navigate the complexities of life together."

Their hearts brimming with hope and anticipation, they seal their promise with a tender kiss. In that fleeting moment, the world fades away, leaving only the two of them standing on the precipice of a beautiful future.

CHAPTER 5: HEART-TO-HEART

Alice and Sherlock found respite from the clamor of the show in a peaceful park, nestled within nature's embrace. They strolled along a winding path, the soft rustling of leaves and the gentle lapping of water from the nearby lake creating a soothing symphony. The park exuded a sense of tranquility, the perfect backdrop for the heartfelt conversation that awaited them.

They settled on a weathered wooden bench, overlooking the serene lake. The warm sunlight filtered through the canopy of trees, casting dappled shadows on their faces. It was a moment of serenity, a pause in their hectic lives that allowed them to connect on a deeper level.

As they sat side by side, the gentle breeze carrying a hint of floral fragrance, Alice and Sherlock exchanged shy smiles. They felt a shared sense of ease in each other's presence, a comfort that transcended the boundaries of their individual worlds.

The stillness of the surroundings mirrored the calmness in their hearts as they began to open up to one another. Their eyes met, and they took a collective breath, ready to embark on a journey of emotional discovery.

The park became a sanctuary, a safe haven where they could speak their truths without reservation. The outside world faded away, leaving only the connection between them. It was in this tranquil setting that they would reveal their dreams, their fears, and the desires that lay dormant within their hearts.

The air seemed charged with anticipation, as if the park itself held its breath, eager to witness the depth of their connection unfold.

The soft rustling of leaves became an encouraging whisper, urging them to open their hearts and let the conversation flow.

In this serene setting, Alice and Sherlock began to delve into their innermost thoughts and aspirations. Their voices carried a mixture of vulnerability and excitement, filling the air with a blend of laughter, sighs, and shared moments of contemplation. The park seemed to listen, absorbing their words and holding them in its embrace.

As the heartfelt conversation unfolded, the bond between them deepened. They discovered common dreams and aspirations, realizing that their paths had converged for a reason. The park bore witness to their blossoming connection, a connection that held the promise of a beautiful future.

As they settled into the comforting embrace of the park, Alice and Sherlock embarked on a journey of shared passions and heartfelt revelations. Their conversation flowed effortlessly, like the rippling waters of the nearby lake, as they delved into the depths of their literary souls.

Alice's eyes lit up as she spoke about her favorite authors, the ones who had shaped her perspective on life and ignited her love for literature. She recounted the profound impact of Jane Austen's works, how the themes of love, social class, and personal growth had resonated with her on a profound level. Sherlock listened intently, captivated by the way her voice carried a mix of reverence and enthusiasm.

In turn, Sherlock shared his own literary musings, revealing his penchant for crime fiction and the psychological complexities that drew him to the genre. He spoke of Sir Arthur Conan Doyle's Sherlock Holmes stories, the intricate puzzles and deductive reasoning that had fascinated him since childhood. Alice hung on his every word, finding herself spellbound by his passion and the layers of depth he revealed.

Their conversation meandered through the corridors of time, touching upon the works of F. Scott Fitzgerald, Toni Morrison, and countless others who had left an indelible mark on their literary journeys. They shared their interpretations, debated the nuances of characters and plotlines, and discovered new layers of understanding within the pages of beloved books.

In their shared love for literature, Alice and Sherlock found solace and inspiration. The park became their literary sanctuary, a space where their hearts could roam free, unburdened by the challenges of reality. They connected through the power of words, finding a profound understanding and a mutual appreciation for the transformative magic of storytelling.

As the sun cast its golden hues over the park, Alice and Sherlock reveled in the beauty of their connection. Their conversation had transcended the ordinary, opening doors to a world of shared dreams and aspirations. They discovered that their love for literature was just one facet of the multifaceted bond that was growing between them.

In that tranquil setting, surrounded by the whispers of nature and the unspoken promises of their hearts, Alice and Sherlock forged a deeper connection. Their shared passion for literature became a stepping stone towards unraveling the intricacies of their own story, and as they continued their conversation, they realized that the chapters they were writing together were even more captivating than the books they held dear.

As the conversation wove its way through the tapestry of literature, Alice and Sherlock found themselves tiptoeing closer to the vulnerable corners of their hearts. With each shared insight into their favorite books, they revealed fragments of their past hurts and the lingering scars that shaped their present.

Alice hesitated for a moment, her gaze fixed on the distant horizon, before summoning the courage to share her deepest fears and vulnerabilities. She spoke of the loss of her husband, the void that still echoed in her heart, and the fear of opening herself up to love again. She confessed how the weight of her responsibilities as a single mother sometimes made her doubt her own capacity for happiness.

Sherlock's eyes softened with empathy, recognizing the pain in Alice's voice. In response, he opened up about his own struggles, the ghosts that haunted his thoughts in the stillness of the night. He spoke of the profound grief that had consumed him after the loss of his wife, the fear of being unable to provide his son with the love and stability he deserved. Through the veil of vulnerability, he revealed the intricate tapestry of emotions that defined his journey.

In this sacred space they had created, Alice and Sherlock found solace in each other's stories. They listened with unwavering attention, offering silent support and understanding. The weight of their shared pain was halved as they discovered the healing power of empathy, realizing that their individual battles were not fought alone.

Together, they acknowledged the complexity of healing and the importance of allowing oneself to feel and process emotions. They recognized that their scars did not define them, but instead shaped them into the resilient individuals they had become. And in each other's presence, they found the strength to peel back the layers of their past and embrace the possibility of a future filled with love and growth.

The park, once a serene backdrop to their conversation, now became a sanctuary of healing. The gentle breeze whispered words of encouragement, and the rustling leaves seemed to offer reassurance that their shared journey of healing was not one they had to face alone.

As the sun dipped below the horizon, casting a warm, golden glow over Alice and Sherlock, they found comfort in the knowledge that their connection went beyond shared passions and literary musings. They had discovered a safe harbor within each other's hearts, a place where vulnerability was met with compassion and scars were embraced as part of a shared narrative.

In the embrace of vulnerability and understanding, Alice and Sherlock realized that they were not just two individuals trying to heal; they were two souls intertwining their stories, finding solace and strength in their shared vulnerabilities. With each heartfelt revelation, they grew closer, their hearts knitting together a tapestry of resilience and hope.

With each shared tale of triumph and resilience, Alice and Sherlock became steadfast pillars of support for one another. They celebrated each other's victories, no matter how small, and offered words of encouragement in times of doubt. In this sacred space they had created, they became cheerleaders for each other's dreams and champions of their inherent worth.

Alice marveled at Sherlock's unwavering dedication to his passion for criminology, recognizing the brilliance that emanated from his every word. She reminded him of the profound impact he had on his students and the valuable contributions he made to the field. Through her heartfelt encouragement, she helped rekindle his belief in himself and the importance of pursuing his dreams.

Sherlock, in turn, marveled at Alice's boundless passion for literature and her ability to inspire her students with her love for books. He saw the fire in her eyes as she spoke about the transformative power of storytelling and the joy she derived from connecting with her students. He reminded her of the profound influence she had on shaping young minds and the difference she made in their lives.

In the depths of their connection, Alice and Sherlock recognized the importance of holding space for each other's dreams and aspirations. They understood that true love was not about eclipsing one another, but rather about lifting each other higher and encouraging the pursuit of individual passions. Together, they kindled a flame of belief, reminding each other of their inherent worth and the limitless possibilities that awaited them.

Their words became beacons of strength, resonating deep within their souls. They formed a sacred pact to support each other, not just in their shared journey but in their individual pursuits as well. They vowed to be each other's rock, providing a safe space for vulnerability and fostering an environment where dreams could flourish.

As they basked in the warmth of their connection, Alice and Sherlock found solace in knowing that they were not alone in their quest for personal fulfillment. They had discovered a partner who not only understood their dreams but celebrated them with unwavering enthusiasm. With each word of encouragement, they built a foundation of mutual respect and unwavering support.

In the backdrop of their conversations, the world seemed to whisper its approval. The trees swayed in harmony, as if applauding their commitment to nurture each other's dreams. The universe, too, seemed to conspire in their favor, aligning the stars to guide them towards a future where they could chase their dreams hand in hand.

As the sun cast its golden rays upon them, Alice and Sherlock stood together, their hearts overflowing with gratitude for the profound connection they had forged. They knew that, with their unwavering support and belief in each other, they would soar to new heights and unlock the doors to a world where dreams became reality.

With their hearts brimming with newfound hope and the weight of vulnerability momentarily lifted, Alice and Sherlock embraced the joyous spirit of the moment. They reveled in the simplicity of life's pleasures, finding solace in each other's company.

As they strolled along the edge of the lake, Alice and Sherlock noticed a cluster of ducks gracefully gliding through the water. With mischievous smiles, they decided to join in the whimsy of the moment. Hand in hand, they approached the ducks, extending their hands to offer small morsels of bread. The ducks flocked around them, their quacks blending with the sounds of laughter and pure delight.

Lost in the enchantment of the scene, Alice and Sherlock found themselves caught up in a spontaneous dance. With the wind rustling through the leaves above and the faint sound of music playing in their hearts, they twirled and spun, their laughter echoing through the park. The world around them seemed to fade into the background as they surrendered themselves to the magic of the moment.

With each twirl and twinkle in their eyes, they forged memories that would forever be etched in their hearts. The weight of their pasts lifted, replaced by a profound connection and a shared joy that enveloped them. They were free, free to be their authentic selves, to dance with abandon, and to revel in the simplicity of being alive.

In that shared dance, Alice and Sherlock discovered a deeper layer of intimacy. They found comfort in their ability to be carefree and vulnerable with one another. Their laughter became a symphony, echoing the unspoken language of their souls. In that moment, they realized that love wasn't just about healing wounds and sharing burdens; it was also about finding joy and creating beautiful memories together.

As the sun dipped below the horizon, casting a warm golden glow over their playful embrace, Alice and Sherlock held each other close, cherishing the simplicity and beauty of the moment. They were reminded that love, in all its forms, had the power to heal, inspire, and create moments of pure bliss.

With their hearts intertwined and their spirits lifted, Alice and Sherlock knew that their journey had taken an enchanting turn.

In each other's presence, they had discovered a reservoir of joy that would sustain them through the trials and tribulations yet to come. Hand in hand, they continued to dance, embracing the magic that had enveloped their lives, as they ventured into a future filled with love, laughter, and cherished memories.

In that blissful moment, surrounded by the serenity of the park, Alice and Sherlock felt a profound shift within their souls. They gazed into each other's eyes, recognizing the profound truth that happiness resides in the present moment.

They both carried scars from their pasts, wounds that had shaped them and left lingering doubts. The weight of regrets and the uncertainty of the future had often clouded their minds. But as they held hands and shared a deep, heartfelt connection, they realized that the beauty of life unfolded in the simplicity of being together.

Alice let out a contented sigh, her worries melting away as she found solace in the warmth of Sherlock's presence. "Sherlock," she whispered, her voice filled with a mixture of gratitude and determination, "I've spent so much of my life dwelling on the past or worrying about the future. But in this moment, with you, I feel a profound sense of peace. Let's embrace the beauty of now and not let regrets or uncertainties hold us back."

Sherlock's eyes gleamed with understanding and a newfound sense of clarity. "Alice, you've voiced the very thoughts that have echoed in my heart. We cannot change the past, nor can we control what lies ahead. But we have the power to choose how we embrace the present, how we make each moment count. Let's savor this connection we've discovered and cherish the beauty of our togetherness."

As they embraced, the weight of past disappointments and future anxieties lifted. They made a conscious decision to release the burdens that no longer served them, allowing themselves to fully immerse in the love and joy that enveloped them.

In the sanctuary of the park, Alice and Sherlock found solace in the simplicity of shared moments. They reveled in the gentle breeze caressing their skin, the symphony of nature's sounds, and the feeling of their hearts beating in sync. Each passing second became a precious gift, a reminder to treasure the here and now.

With every shared laugh, every gentle touch, and every stolen glance, Alice and Sherlock nurtured their connection. They basked in the serendipity that had brought them together and promised to make the most of every precious second they were given.

In that moment of realization, Alice and Sherlock discovered that true happiness wasn't anchored in the past or reliant on the future. It resided in the present, in the unconditional love and acceptance they found in each other's arms.

With open hearts and minds unburdened by regrets or uncertainties, Alice and Sherlock vowed to live each day fully, embracing the beauty of the present and reveling in the magic of their connection. The park became a symbol of their shared commitment to savor the simple joys of life, and with each step they took, they found themselves walking towards a future where happiness bloomed in every moment spent together.

As the sun began its descent, casting a warm golden glow over their surroundings, Alice and Sherlock held each other tightly, knowing that their journey was far from over. With hearts overflowing with gratitude and a renewed appreciation for the power of now, they walked hand in hand, ready to embrace the adventures and challenges that lay ahead.

As the sun began to set, painting the sky in hues of pink and orange, Alice and Sherlock found themselves lost in the realm of their shared dreams. Their hearts, brimming with hope and a sense of newfound clarity, yearned for a future filled with love, adventure, and endless possibilities.

Alice gazed at the horizon, her voice filled with a quiet determination. "Sherlock, I can't help but imagine the life we could build together. A life filled with laughter, shared adventures, and a love that grows stronger with each passing day. I want to explore the world hand in hand, uncovering hidden treasures and creating memories that will last a lifetime."

Sherlock's eyes sparkled with anticipation, his voice laced with a gentle enthusiasm. "Alice, the thought of embarking on grand adventures with you by my side fills me with a profound sense of excitement. I want to dive into the depths of mystery and unravel the enigmas that lie before us. I envision a life where we challenge each other, inspire growth, and support one another's wildest aspirations."

They shared a knowing smile, their dreams intertwining and merging into a shared vision. It was a future where love and adventure danced hand in hand, where they would seize every opportunity that came their way and fearlessly embrace the unknown.

In that moment, the park transformed into a sanctuary of possibilities, a space where their dreams could take flight. The gentle rustle of leaves whispered promises of a life lived to the fullest, of hearts entwined and souls aligned.

As they stood side by side, the warmth of their connection enveloping them, Alice and Sherlock pledged to nurture their dreams and turn them into realities. They vowed to support each other's growth, encouraging one another to step outside their comfort zones and explore the depths of their potential.

The future shimmered with a sense of optimism, like an uncharted path waiting to be discovered. They knew it wouldn't always be smooth sailing, that challenges and obstacles would inevitably arise. But together, they were ready to face whatever lay ahead, their love and unwavering commitment as their guiding light.

With hearts brimming with hope, Alice and Sherlock took a moment to savor the magic of the present, the love that bound them, and the dreams that beckoned them forward. They knew that their connection was evolving into something beautiful, a love story that would transcend time and leave an indelible mark on their lives.

As the last rays of sunlight bathed the park in a golden glow, Alice and Sherlock shared a tender embrace, their dreams entwined with their hearts. They stepped into the future hand in hand, ready to chase their dreams, write their own love story, and embrace the adventure that awaited them.

CHAPTER 6: UNEXPECTED OBSTACLES

The TV studio buzzed with energy as Alice and Sherlock returned after their intimate conversation. The air crackled with anticipation, blending with the familiar hum of cameras, bustling crew members, and the faint echo of conversations. The set, once again, became their stage, but this time, they couldn't ignore the lingering effects of their heartfelt connection.

Alice adjusted her blouse, feeling a mixture of excitement and apprehension coursing through her veins. She stole a glance at Sherlock, who stood beside her, his face a portrait of calm composure. The weight of their previous conversation still lingered, threading an invisible bond between them.

The set was a whirlwind of activity, as crew members hurriedly prepared for the next challenge. Equipment was being adjusted, props were positioned, and the cameras stood ready to capture the unfolding drama. Alice and Sherlock exchanged a brief smile, silently acknowledging the unspoken promise of support that lay between them.

As they watched the host, Emily, move across the set, her infectious energy infusing the room, Alice couldn't help but feel a flutter of nervous excitement. What would the next challenge entail? What obstacles would they face? Unbeknownst to them, the path ahead would test their commitment and resilience in ways they couldn't yet imagine.

Sherlock's eyes scanned the studio, his analytical mind taking in every detail. He observed the crew members with their focused determination and the set, transformed once again into a stage for their journey. Deep down, he knew that the upcoming challenge would push them further, both individually and as a pair. Yet, he also felt a newfound sense of confidence, fueled by the connection he shared with Alice.

The anticipation in the air was palpable, mingling with a hint of uncertainty. Alice and Sherlock took a moment to steady themselves, finding solace in the familiarity of the TV studio. They were ready to face whatever awaited them, to embrace the challenge and grow stronger together.

Little did they know, this next obstacle would test not only their physical abilities but also their emotional resilience. As they prepared to dive headfirst into the unknown, their hearts beat in unison, anchored by a shared determination to overcome whatever lay ahead. The stage was set, and Alice and Sherlock stood poised on the precipice of another transformative chapter in their journey on the show.

Emily's voice boomed through the studio, drawing the attention of Alice and Sherlock. She wore a mischievous smile, a glint of excitement dancing in her eyes. "Ladies and gentlemen, I have an announcement to make," she declared, her voice carrying a hint of mystery.

The room fell silent, the crew members pausing their tasks to listen intently. Alice and Sherlock exchanged a quick glance, their eyes reflecting a mix of curiosity and apprehension. A sense of unease crept into their hearts, wondering what unexpected twist awaited them.

"Today's challenge," Emily continued, her voice tinged with theatrical flair, "will test your ability to confront your deepest fears and insecurities."

Alice's breath caught in her throat, her mind swirling with a rush of thoughts and uncertainties. She had faced many challenges in her life, but this was different. It was one thing to confront physical obstacles, but to delve into the depths of her own fears felt overwhelming.

Sherlock's brow furrowed, his analytical mind racing to anticipate the kind of challenge that lay ahead. As a man driven by logic and reason, the idea of confronting his own insecurities stirred a subtle discomfort within him. He prided himself on his ability to maintain composure, but this challenge threatened to shake that facade.

Emily continued, her voice laden with encouragement, "Remember, this challenge is an opportunity for personal growth, to conquer what holds you back. It will require vulnerability and courage. But trust in yourselves and in each other, and you may discover newfound strength."

Alice and Sherlock exchanged another glance, a silent communication passing between them. The weight of the task ahead pressed upon their shoulders, threatening to unravel the confidence they had built. Doubts seeped into their minds, questioning whether their connection was strong enough to endure this unexpected twist.

In that moment, their eyes met, and a silent understanding passed between them. They recognized the fears mirrored in each other's gaze, but they also glimpsed the unyielding determination that had brought them this far. It was a reminder of the depth of their connection, the strength they drew from one another.

As Emily concluded her announcement, the studio erupted with a mix of excitement and nervous energy. Alice and Sherlock took a deep breath, their resolve firming within them. They may not have known the precise nature of the challenge that awaited them, but they were ready to face it together, their bond fortified by the shared desire to conquer their fears and insecurities.

In this unexpected twist, Alice and Sherlock found solace in the knowledge that they would not face these trials alone. With their hearts entwined, they would support each other through the storm, their connection a beacon of strength in the face of uncertainty. As the stage was set for this new test, they held onto the belief that love, courage, and their unwavering bond would guide them through whatever challenges lay ahead.

In the secluded corner of the studio, away from prying eyes and the clamor of the ongoing production, Alice and Sherlock found a brief respite. Silence enveloped them, allowing their racing thoughts to find a momentary refuge.

Alice stared into the distance, her brow furrowed with concern. The unexpected twist in the show had stirred a whirlwind of doubts within her. The fear of exposing her vulnerabilities, of confronting the shadows that lurked in the depths of her being, threatened to erode the foundation they had built.

Sherlock leaned against the wall, his gaze fixed on a distant point. His analytical mind was working furiously, dissecting the potential implications of the upcoming challenge. He was no stranger to facing his fears, but the thought of revealing his deepest insecurities to a broader audience filled him with a trepidation he rarely allowed himself to acknowledge.

The weight of uncertainty settled upon them, its presence casting a shadow over the warmth of their connection. They had come so far, their bond growing with each passing day, but now the path ahead seemed shrouded in fog.

Alice spoke first, her voice tinged with vulnerability. "Sherlock, I can't help but worry about what this challenge means for us. Will our connection be strong enough to withstand the tests that await?"

Sherlock turned his gaze towards Alice, his eyes filled with a mix of empathy and determination. "Alice, I understand your concerns. It's only natural to question the strength of our bond in the face of such uncertainty. But remember, it's in these moments of vulnerability that we find our truest selves."

Alice nodded, a glimmer of hope flickering in her eyes. "You're right, Sherlock. We have come this far because we trust in each other, because we have supported one another through the challenges we've faced. We must hold onto that trust and face this new test together."

Sherlock reached out and gently took Alice's hand, his touch a reassurance of their shared commitment. "We have built something special, Alice. Our connection is rooted in understanding, trust, and unwavering support. Let us not allow doubt to cast shadows upon what we have."

As they stood there, hand in hand, a renewed sense of determination welled up within them. They understood that their journey was not meant to be free of challenges, but it was through facing those challenges head-on that their connection would deepen and flourish.

In the face of uncertainty, Alice and Sherlock chose to anchor themselves in the belief that their bond was resilient, capable of weathering any storm. With hearts intertwined, they steeled themselves for the upcoming test, ready to confront their fears and insecurities, knowing that together they were stronger than any doubts that may arise.

As they stepped back into the bustling energy of the studio, their eyes met, and a silent understanding passed between them. The path ahead may be uncertain, but their commitment to each other remained steadfast. Hand in hand, they were ready to face the challenge, united in their unwavering love and the shared purpose of growth and self-discovery.

As they bared their vulnerabilities to one another, Alice and Sherlock discovered the immense power of their shared honesty. Their doubts and fears were no longer burdens to carry alone, but hurdles they could overcome together.

Alice looked into Sherlock's eyes, her voice laced with a newfound determination. "Sherlock, we've faced adversity before, and we've emerged stronger each time. This challenge may be daunting, but I have unwavering faith in us. Together, we can conquer anything."

Sherlock's gaze softened, his voice filled with conviction. "Alice, you're right. Our connection has grown amidst the trials we've faced. We have proven time and again that we are a formidable team. Let's draw strength from our shared experiences and face this challenge head-on."

With their worries temporarily quelled, Alice and Sherlock returned to the bustling set with a renewed sense of purpose. They held onto the knowledge that their bond was fortified by resilience and the unwavering belief they had in each other.

As they joined the rest of the cast and crew, the air crackled with a palpable energy. The challenge loomed ahead, an unknown entity testing their limits. But Alice and Sherlock, hand in hand, faced it with a newfound courage, ready to confront their fears and emerge stronger on the other side.

The cameras began to roll, capturing every emotion, every obstacle they would encounter. Alice and Sherlock drew strength from their connection, relying on their shared understanding and unwavering support to navigate the twists and turns of the challenge.

Together, they faced their fears head-on, their determination radiating like a beacon in the darkness. They pushed each other to surpass their own expectations, their bond growing stronger with every hurdle they overcame.

In the midst of the challenge, Alice and Sherlock found solace in the fact that they were not alone in their struggles. They drew inspiration from one another's tenacity, their unwavering support guiding them through even the toughest moments.

As the challenge drew to a close, Alice and Sherlock stood side by side, their faces flushed with triumph. They had conquered their fears, proving once again that their connection was unyielding. The doubt that had clouded their minds dissipated, replaced by a renewed belief in the power of their love.

With a shared smile, they celebrated their victory, embracing the knowledge that their bond was resilient, capable of withstanding any obstacle. As they left the set, hand in hand, they carried with them a profound sense of unity, ready to face whatever challenges lay ahead, knowing that together they were an unstoppable force.

Their journey had only just begun, and with each challenge they conquered, Alice and Sherlock grew closer, their love blossoming amidst the trials and triumphs of their shared adventure.
Alice and Sherlock retreated to a secluded corner of the studio, their minds buzzing with anticipation. They knew that the upcoming challenge required not only courage but also strategic thinking. They took a seat, facing each other, ready to dive into the planning process.

Alice opened her notebook, flipping through the pages filled with meticulous notes and ideas. "Sherlock, we need to leverage our individual strengths to overcome this obstacle. Let's analyze the challenge and come up with a plan that maximizes our chances of success."

Sherlock nodded, his gaze focused and determined. "Absolutely, Alice. We need to identify the key elements of the challenge and find ways to use our skills to our advantage. Together, we can outsmart any hurdle that comes our way."

They began dissecting the details of the challenge, analyzing its components and potential pitfalls. With each passing minute, their confidence grew, fueled by the knowledge that they had each other's unwavering support.

Alice pointed to a diagram on her notebook, outlining a potential solution. "What if we combine your exceptional observation skills with my ability to think on my feet? We can create a strategy that allows us to anticipate obstacles and respond swiftly."

Sherlock's eyes lit up with excitement. "Yes, and we can also incorporate your creative problem-solving skills and my logical reasoning to tackle any unexpected twists that may arise. Our combined intellect will be our greatest asset."

They continued to bounce ideas off each other, drawing from their shared experiences and unique perspectives. They found themselves entering a state of flow, their minds synchronized in a dance of innovation and collaboration.

As the planning session unfolded, Alice and Sherlock became acutely aware of how their individual strengths complemented each other. They realized that their connection extended beyond their emotional bond; it was a partnership built on mutual respect and admiration.

With their strategy solidified and their confidence restored, Alice and Sherlock stood up, ready to face the challenge head-on. They shared a knowing smile, their determination radiating from within.

As they rejoined the rest of the participants on the set, Alice and Sherlock carried with them a renewed sense of purpose. They were ready to embrace the challenge, armed with a well-thought-out plan and the unwavering belief in their abilities.

Little did they know that the obstacle they were about to face would push them to their limits, testing not only their individual strengths but also the depth of their connection. But they were prepared, knowing that together they were an unstoppable force.

As the cameras started rolling, capturing every moment of their journey, Alice and Sherlock stepped forward, their hearts filled with determination. They were ready to conquer the challenge, knowing that no matter what lay ahead, they would face it as a united front.

With their strategy in place and their bond unbreakable, Alice and Sherlock embarked on the next phase of their adventure, ready to overcome whatever obstacles stood in their way.

As the tension in the studio reached its peak, the host, Emily, stepped forward, holding an envelope in her hand. The room fell silent, every pair of eyes fixed on her.

"Contestants, the time has come for the unveiling of the next challenge," Emily announced, her voice filled with a mix of excitement and gravity. "This challenge will test your trust, your resilience, and your ability to confront your deepest fears."

Alice and Sherlock exchanged a nervous glance, their hearts pounding in unison. They knew that this challenge would push them to their limits, requiring them to confront their vulnerabilities head-on.

Emily opened the envelope and read aloud, "Contestants, you will be blindfolded and led to a series of physical obstacles. You must rely on your partner's guidance and trust them completely to navigate through the course."

A gasp rippled through the room, and Alice felt a surge of adrenaline course through her veins. Blindfolded? Trusting someone else to guide her through unknown obstacles? It was a test of both physical and emotional strength.

Sherlock's eyes met Alice's, their determination unwavering. They knew that this challenge was not only about overcoming physical obstacles but also about confronting their own fears and insecurities.

Alice took a deep breath, mustering her courage. "Sherlock, we've faced challenges before, and we've come out stronger. I trust you, and I believe in our connection. We can do this together."

Sherlock nodded, his voice filled with conviction. "Alice, I trust you as well. We will navigate this challenge, step by step, relying on our instincts and the trust we have built. We won't let anything come between us."

As they prepared for the blindfolding process, Alice and Sherlock tightened their grip on each other's hands, drawing strength from the physical connection they shared. They focused on their breathing, calming their nerves, and preparing themselves mentally for what lay ahead.

Blindfolded and led by the show's assistants, Alice and Sherlock stepped onto the course. Every step was a leap of faith, every obstacle a test of their trust in one another.

Alice's heart raced as she felt Sherlock's steady hand guiding her through each challenge. She listened to his voice, his calm and reassuring tone providing a beacon of hope in the darkness.

Sherlock's keen observation skills came to the forefront as he analyzed the surroundings, making split-second decisions to keep them on the right path. He trusted his instincts, relying on his bond with Alice to guide them through the unknown.

With every obstacle they conquered together, their trust in each other grew. They felt their connection deepen, the bond forged through shared vulnerability and unwavering support.

As they neared the end of the challenge, their blindfolds were finally removed, revealing a triumphant smile on Alice's face and a sense of accomplishment in Sherlock's eyes. They had faced their fears, conquered the obstacles, and emerged stronger than ever.

Alice and Sherlock stood side by side, their hands still intertwined, their hearts brimming with pride. They had proved to themselves and to the world that their trust and belief in each other could overcome even the most daunting challenges.

As the studio erupted in applause, Alice and Sherlock shared a knowing look, their connection unbreakable. They had triumphed over their deepest fears, and the road ahead was filled with endless possibilities.

Little did they know that this challenge was just the beginning of their journey, a stepping stone to even greater trials and triumphs. They were ready to face whatever lay ahead, knowing that together, they could conquer anything.

With the challenge behind them and their trust strengthened, Alice and Sherlock were prepared to embrace the next chapter of their adventure, eager to explore the depths of their connection and the love that had blossomed between them.
With their blindfolds securely in place, Alice and Sherlock stood at the entrance of the obstacle course. Their hearts beat in unison, anticipation coursing through their veins. Gripping each other's hands tightly, they exchanged a wordless vow to face this challenge together.

As the first step into the unknown, Alice felt her pulse quicken. Darkness surrounded her, heightening her senses and forcing her to rely solely on Sherlock's guidance. She trusted him implicitly, allowing his steady voice to be her guiding light.

"Step forward, Alice," Sherlock's voice resonated with confidence. "There's a small incline ahead, but I'll be right here with you."

Alice took a deep breath, summoning her courage, and placed her foot on the inclined platform. With Sherlock's guidance, she ascended, feeling the strain in her muscles but also the unwavering support of her partner.

They encountered unexpected challenges along the way—narrow beams to balance on, rope nets to crawl through, and dark tunnels to navigate. Each obstacle tested their physical and emotional strength, demanding trust and reliance on one another.

In moments of doubt, Alice and Sherlock found solace in their connection. They encouraged each other, their voices blending harmoniously in the darkness. They reassured one another that they were capable, reminding each other of their individual strengths and the power of their partnership.

With each obstacle conquered, their trust in each other deepened. The blindfolds that had initially limited their vision became a symbol of their unwavering belief in each other. They embraced the challenge as an opportunity to not only face their fears but to grow stronger together.

As they reached the final obstacle—a wall to scale—Alice hesitated for a moment, her fingers gripping the rough surface. Doubt whispered in her ear, but she found strength in Sherlock's unwavering presence beside her.

"You can do this, Alice," Sherlock's voice carried conviction. "I'm right here with you, ready to catch you if you fall."

With a surge of determination, Alice propelled herself upward, her muscles straining with effort. Sherlock followed closely behind, providing encouragement and guidance. Together, they conquered the wall, ascending to victory.

As they stood atop the wall, their blindfolds were gently removed, revealing a breathtaking view before them. They gazed at each other, their eyes reflecting triumph and a newfound resilience. In that moment, they realized the depth of their trust, their unwavering support for one another, and the unbreakable bond they had forged.

The studio erupted in applause, celebrating their triumph and the strength of their partnership. Alice and Sherlock basked in the acknowledgment, their hearts swelling with pride and joy. They had faced their fears head-on and emerged victorious, stronger than ever before.

As they made their way back to the center of the studio, hand in hand, Alice and Sherlock knew that this challenge had tested their trust and resilience in unimaginable ways. They had discovered the depth of their connection, the power of their unwavering support, and the indomitable spirit that fueled their partnership.

Little did they know, the obstacles they had faced were merely a prelude to the challenges and adventures that awaited them. With their trust solidified and their bond fortified, Alice and Sherlock were ready to take on whatever the future had in store, knowing that together, they could conquer anything that came their way. As Alice and Sherlock stood on the other side of the obstacle, their breaths ragged and their bodies adorned with sweat, a triumphant smile lit up their faces. They had conquered the challenge, defying their fears and proving the strength of their partnership.

In the wake of their victory, a sense of euphoria enveloped them. They embraced each other, their hearts pounding in synchrony. The weight of the challenge lifted from their shoulders, replaced by a profound sense of accomplishment and a deeper appreciation for what they were capable of achieving together.

Their shared victory created a bond that was unbreakable, solidifying their trust and reinforcing their belief in each other. Alice and Sherlock reveled in the moment, savoring the joy that radiated between them. Their journey on the show had become more than just a competition—it had become a testament to their resilience and the power of their connection.

As the applause from the crew and fellow contestants echoed in the studio, Alice and Sherlock exchanged knowing glances. They had faced their fears head-on, proving that they were more than the sum of their individual strengths. Their triumph had not only brought them closer but had ignited a fire within them, a desire to continue pushing boundaries and seizing every opportunity that lay ahead.

In the midst of their celebration, Alice leaned in, her voice filled with gratitude and admiration. "Sherlock, I couldn't have done this without you. Your unwavering support and belief in me gave me the strength to overcome my doubts."

Sherlock's eyes gleamed with pride as he responded, "And I, Alice, owe much of my courage to your unwavering determination and unwavering spirit. You have shown me the power of trust and the beauty of vulnerability."

They stood there, basking in the glow of their victory and the warmth of their shared affection. In that moment, Alice and Sherlock knew that their connection went beyond the boundaries of the show. It was a connection rooted in mutual respect, understanding, and a profound love that had blossomed amidst the challenges they had faced together.

As they prepared for the next phase of the show, Alice and Sherlock held on to the memories of their triumph. They carried with them the knowledge that, no matter what obstacles lay ahead, they were an unstoppable team—two hearts intertwined, ready to face whatever came their way.

Little did they know, the challenges that awaited them would test their bond in even greater ways. But with the strength they had found in each other and the unwavering belief that they were meant to be, Alice and Sherlock were prepared to face whatever lay ahead, confident that their love would guide them through any storm.

Together, they stepped forward, ready to embrace the next chapter of their journey, hand in hand, and heart to heart.
As the applause subsided and the studio began to quiet down, a hushed whisper spread among the contestants and crew. Emily, the host, stepped forward with a mischievous smile playing on her lips.

"Congratulations, Alice and Sherlock," she said, her voice tinged with excitement. "You have proven yourselves to be a formidable team. But get ready, because the next challenge will push your bond to its limits."

Alice and Sherlock exchanged a curious glance, their hearts

pounding with a mix of anticipation and trepidation. What new obstacle awaited them? What test would they have to face now?

Emily continued, her eyes gleaming with intrigue. "In the next challenge, you will be separated and placed in different locations. You'll have to rely on your instincts, communication, and unwavering trust in each other to reunite. Can your connection withstand the distance? Can your love guide you back to each other?"

The air crackled with uncertainty as Alice and Sherlock absorbed the magnitude of the upcoming challenge. Their commitment to each other was about to be tested like never before, and the stakes had never been higher.

With determined expressions, they locked eyes once again, silently vowing to face this new trial head-on. Their bond had grown stronger with each obstacle they had conquered, and they believed in their love's ability to transcend any physical separation.

As they prepared themselves mentally and emotionally for the upcoming challenge, Alice and Sherlock took solace in the unwavering support they had found in each other. They knew that no matter what lay ahead, their connection was unbreakable, and their love would guide them back into each other's arms.

The chapter ended with a tantalizing cliffhanger, leaving the reader on the edge of their seat, eagerly anticipating how Alice and Sherlock would navigate the challenge and whether their love would prove strong enough to reunite them.

Little did they know, this next test would push their boundaries in ways they never imagined, and their journey would take an unexpected turn that would change the course of their lives forever.

CHAPTER 7: THE JOURNEY OF THEIR HEARTS

The air inside the TV studio crackled with electricity as Alice and Sherlock returned to the set after their intimate conversation. They found themselves amidst the controlled chaos of cameras, crew members scurrying about, and the low murmur of excited voices. The energy was palpable, a mix of anticipation and nervous excitement, as everyone prepared for the next challenge.

Alice adjusted her hair and straightened her clothing, her heart beating a little faster. She stole a glance at Sherlock, who stood nearby, composed and focused. There was a sense of determination in his eyes, a quiet resolve that mirrored her own.

Around them, the crew members hurriedly set up equipment, ensuring everything was in place for the upcoming challenge. The lights overhead cast a bright glow, casting dramatic shadows on the set. The stage had been transformed into an elaborate obstacle course, a physical and mental trial waiting to be conquered.

As the countdown to the challenge began, Alice and Sherlock exchanged a brief, knowing glance. Their connection felt even stronger after their heartfelt conversation, and they were ready to face whatever awaited them.

Emily, the show's host, stood at the center of the set, microphone in hand. Her energy was infectious as she rallied the audience, building anticipation for the next thrilling chapter of the show. She spoke of resilience, teamwork, and the power of love.

Alice and Sherlock took a deep breath, their eyes locked on each other, finding solace and strength in their shared determination. They had come so far together, and they were ready to take on whatever obstacles lay ahead.

As Emily signaled for the challenge to begin, Alice and Sherlock stepped forward, their hands almost instinctively finding each other's. They were about to embark on another journey, one that would test not only their physical abilities but also their emotional connection.

Little did they know that this challenge would push them to their limits, forcing them to confront their deepest fears and insecurities. The studio fell into a hushed silence, the only sound echoing through the air was the beating of their hearts, intertwined as they faced the unknown.

The stage was set, the clock ticking, and Alice and Sherlock stood together, ready to take on the next chapter of their adventure. With a shared resolve and unyielding determination, they stepped into the unknown, their hearts filled with hope and the promise of a love that could overcome any obstacle.

As the excitement in the studio reached its peak, Emily, the charismatic host, stepped forward, a mischievous smile playing on her lips. The audience leaned in, anticipation hanging in the air, as she revealed a sudden twist that would rock the foundation of the show.

"Dear viewers, dear Alice and Sherlock," Emily's voice boomed through the speakers, "get ready for a challenge unlike anything you've faced before. Today, we will delve into the depths of your fears and insecurities, pushing you to confront the very things that haunt your hearts."

Alice and Sherlock exchanged a surprised yet determined glance. The twist in the show's format caught them off guard, momentarily shaking their confidence. Doubts crept into their minds as they wondered if their connection could withstand the upcoming test. The weight of their individual fears loomed before them, threatening to unravel the bond they had worked so hard to build.

Alice's hands trembled slightly, and Sherlock's brow furrowed with a mix of concern and determination. They had come so far together, but this unexpected challenge would demand vulnerability, courage, and a deep trust in one another.

As the reality of the twist sank in, Alice took a steadying breath, reminding herself of the strength she had discovered within. She turned to Sherlock, her voice filled with a mixture of apprehension and determination. "Sherlock, we've faced challenges before, but this...this will test us in ways we haven't imagined. Can we truly confront our deepest fears and emerge stronger together?"

Sherlock's eyes softened, and he reached out, gently squeezing Alice's hand. "Alice, our connection runs deeper than any obstacle we may face. We've already seen glimpses of our strength, our resilience. Let us trust in ourselves and in each other. Together, we can conquer even the darkest shadows within us."

Their brief exchange, filled with unspoken reassurance and the shared understanding of what lay ahead, helped to restore their wavering confidence. They may have questioned the strength of their connection momentarily, but their bond was built on a solid foundation of trust, empathy, and shared experiences.

With a renewed determination, Alice and Sherlock turned their focus to the challenge that awaited them. They steeled themselves, ready to confront their individual fears head-on, knowing that their connection would be tested like never before.

Little did they know that this unexpected twist would serve as a catalyst for personal growth and a deeper understanding of themselves and each other. As doubts lingered in their minds, they clung to the hope that their love and resilience would carry them through this uncharted territory.

Seeking solace from the chaos surrounding them, Alice and Sherlock found a secluded corner of the bustling studio. They leaned against a nearby wall, their expressions mirroring the weight of their thoughts. The twist in the show's format had ignited a storm of doubts and fears within them, threatening to cast a shadow over the bond they had nurtured.

Alice sighed, her voice laced with uncertainty. "Sherlock, I never anticipated that the show would delve into our deepest fears and insecurities. What if this challenge exposes vulnerabilities we're not ready to confront? Will it strain our connection?"

Sherlock's gaze softened as he reached out to gently grasp Alice's hand. "Alice, it's natural to feel apprehensive in the face of the unknown. But remember, our connection is built on trust and understanding. We have already overcome obstacles together, proving the strength of our bond. This challenge may be daunting, but we will face it together, supporting each other every step of the way."

Alice's eyes searched Sherlock's face, seeking reassurance amidst her swirling doubts. "I believe in us, Sherlock. But what if we discover things about ourselves that we didn't anticipate? Will it change how we see each other?"

Sherlock's voice held unwavering conviction as he replied, "Alice, this challenge is an opportunity for growth, for delving into the depths of who we are. If we face our fears and insecurities honestly, it can only strengthen our bond. Our connection is not built on perfection but on acceptance and understanding. We have the resilience to weather whatever storms lie ahead."

As they stood in that quiet corner of the studio, enveloped by their shared vulnerability, a sense of determination slowly replaced their doubts. They realized that the twists and turns of the show were designed to push them to their limits, to forge a love that was unbreakable.

With renewed resolve, Alice and Sherlock acknowledged the uncertainties and fears that lay ahead. They knew that the journey they embarked on was not without risks, but they were willing to face the challenges head-on, trusting in the strength of their connection and the unwavering support they offered each other.

In the depths of their reflection, they discovered a shared determination to confront their fears and insecurities, knowing that it was through this process that they would grow individually and as a couple. With their hearts intertwined, they were ready to face whatever lay in store, drawing strength from the love they had cultivated and the belief that their bond could withstand any trial.

As doubts threatened to cast a shadow over their bond, Alice and Sherlock found solace in each other's presence. They nestled closer, their bodies seeking comfort and support. With gentle reassurance, they shared their fears and doubts, knowing that vulnerability would only strengthen their connection.

Alice gazed into Sherlock's eyes, her voice filled with sincerity. "Sherlock, I can't help but feel overwhelmed by the challenges ahead. The twist in the show has shaken my confidence. But when I look at you, I see strength and resilience. You've faced adversity with unwavering determination. Together, I believe we can overcome anything."

Sherlock held Alice's gaze, his voice steady and resolute. "Alice, your doubts are valid, and I too find myself questioning our ability to navigate this new challenge. But remember the hurdles we've already conquered. We've shown resilience, adaptability, and a deep understanding of each other. Our connection is not easily broken. It's a source of strength that will guide us through whatever lies ahead."

In the safety of their shared vulnerability, Alice and Sherlock offered each other unwavering support. They encouraged one another to embrace their fears, knowing that true growth came from facing them head-on. With every word of reassurance and every touch of comfort, they reaffirmed their belief in their connection, in the love that had blossomed between them.

As they clung to each other, their doubts began to dissipate, replaced by a renewed sense of confidence. They were reminded that their bond was forged in the crucible of challenges, and it was in those moments that their love had blossomed and flourished.

Together, Alice and Sherlock vowed to lean on each other when doubts resurfaced, to remind one another of their individual strengths and the power of their combined resilience. They would navigate the uncertainty with open hearts and unwavering trust, knowing that their connection could weather any storm.

In that quiet corner of the studio, their fears transformed into determination. They held hands, their fingers intertwined, as they forged a pact to face the upcoming challenge with courage and unwavering support. They were united in their belief that their connection was unshakable and that their love would guide them through the trials yet to come.

With their doubts temporarily silenced, Alice and Sherlock shifted their focus to strategizing for the upcoming challenge. They knew that careful planning and utilizing their individual strengths would be key to their success.

Sitting side by side, they exchanged thoughtful glances, their minds alight with determination. Sherlock initiated the conversation, his voice filled with a mix of intellect and enthusiasm. "Alice, let's assess our strengths and weaknesses. By understanding what we each bring to the table, we can devise a plan that maximizes our potential."

Alice nodded, her eyes sparkling with anticipation. "You're right,

Sherlock. Together, we possess a wealth of skills and talents. Let's start by identifying our individual strengths and how they can complement each other in tackling this challenge."

They spent the next hour engaged in deep discussion, exploring their respective areas of expertise. Sherlock's analytical mind and keen problem-solving abilities were matched by Alice's creativity and intuition. They brainstormed innovative solutions, considering every possible angle and scenario.

Sherlock scribbled notes on a pad of paper, capturing their ideas with precision. "Alice, your ability to think outside the box and approach problems from unique angles is truly remarkable. I believe this will be invaluable in navigating the unexpected twists of the challenge."

Alice smiled, her confidence growing with each word of praise. "And Sherlock, your logical reasoning and attention to detail will be vital in analyzing the intricacies of each task. Your sharp intellect and resourcefulness will undoubtedly guide us through."

As they delved deeper into their planning, the synergy between them became evident. Ideas flowed seamlessly, their thoughts interweaving like a finely choreographed dance. Their combined intellect and resourcefulness sparked a renewed sense of confidence, allowing them to envision success even in the face of uncertainty.

They crafted a strategic plan, dividing tasks based on their individual strengths and assigning roles that played to their abilities. Each step was carefully considered, allowing room for adaptation as the challenge unfolded.

With their plan in place, Alice and Sherlock shared a final look of determination. They knew that challenges lay ahead, but their preparation and shared commitment bolstered their resolve. They were ready to face the obstacle head-on, fortified by their strategic planning and the unbreakable bond that bound them.

With their strategic plan in place, Alice and Sherlock braced themselves for the challenge ahead. The moment of truth arrived as the host, Emily, unveiled the details of the obstacle they were about to face. The challenge was not just a physical test but also an emotional journey that would push them to confront their deepest fears.

Alice's heart pounded in her chest as she listened to Emily's words. She exchanged a nervous glance with Sherlock, their eyes mirroring a mix of determination and apprehension. They understood that this challenge would require them to rely on each other's strength and unwavering support.

Emily's voice resonated through the studio, setting the stage for the daunting task that awaited them. "Alice and Sherlock, the challenge ahead will test your ability to confront your deepest fears. It will require trust, vulnerability, and a willingness to face the unknown together. Are you ready?"

Alice took a deep breath, feeling a surge of adrenaline course through her veins. She turned to Sherlock, her voice filled with determination. "Sherlock, we've come this far, and I believe in our connection. Together, we can conquer anything. Let's face this challenge head-on, knowing that we have each other's backs."

Sherlock's gaze met Alice's, his eyes reflecting unwavering resolve. "Alice, I trust you with my fears, my vulnerabilities. I know that we can rely on each other to navigate this obstacle, just as we have overcome previous challenges. Let's embrace this opportunity for growth and face it together."

As they stepped onto the starting line, Alice and Sherlock shared a silent vow to support each other every step of the way. They were prepared to confront their deepest fears, trusting that their bond would guide them through the darkness and uncertainty.

With hearts pounding and hands tightly clasped, Alice and Sherlock faced the daunting obstacle that stood before them. The air crackled with anticipation as they took their first steps, their eyes locked in a shared determination. Every nerve in their bodies tingled with a mix of excitement and trepidation.

As they delved deeper into the challenge, they encountered unexpected twists and turns that tested their resolve. Doubts crept in, threatening to undermine their confidence, but their unwavering support for each other became their anchor. With every stumble, they provided a steadying hand and words of encouragement, reminding each other of their resilience.

In the face of fear, they discovered newfound strengths within themselves. Alice, known for her determination and unwavering spirit, found a tenacity she never knew existed. Sherlock, often stoic and reserved, tapped into a wellspring of courage that surprised even him. Together, they became a formidable force, pushing each other to greater heights.

Through the challenging moments, their trust in each other deepened. They learned to rely not only on their individual abilities but also on the power of their partnership. Their unbreakable bond allowed them to communicate without words, to understand each other's needs and fears without explanation.

As they overcame each obstacle, their connection grew stronger. They witnessed the incredible support they provided for one another and felt the unwavering belief in their shared journey. Their experiences illuminated the depth of their trust and the undeniable chemistry that existed between them.

In those moments of triumph, Alice and Sherlock stood taller, their spirits soaring. They had conquered not only the physical hurdles but also the emotional barriers that had threatened to derail them. Their resilience had been tested, and they had emerged victorious, basking in the glow of their shared accomplishment.

As Alice and Sherlock crossed the final hurdle of the challenge, a surge of exhilaration washed over them. They stood side by side, panting and smiling, their eyes sparkling with triumph. The weight of the obstacle was lifted, replaced by a profound sense of accomplishment that reverberated through their beings.

In the wake of their victory, Alice and Sherlock took a moment to catch their breath. They looked at each other, their eyes shining with pride and admiration. They shared a knowing smile, an unspoken acknowledgement of the strength they had found in each other.

Unable to contain their joy, they embraced tightly, their hearts beating in sync. The air buzzed with an electric energy, carrying the euphoria of their shared achievement. They reveled in the magnitude of what they had just accomplished, knowing that they had pushed past their limits and emerged stronger than ever before.

In that moment of celebration, Alice and Sherlock cherished the bond they had forged. They relished in the shared moments of triumph and perseverance, the memories that would forever be etched in their hearts. They reveled in the realization that together, they were an unstoppable force, capable of conquering any obstacle that lay in their path.

As they basked in the glow of their victory, Alice and Sherlock knew that their connection had reached a new level. The obstacles they had faced had not only tested their physical and emotional strength but also solidified their belief in the power of their bond. They had witnessed firsthand the unwavering support and unwavering trust they had in each other.

With hearts full and spirits lifted, Alice and Sherlock allowed themselves to revel in the moment. They celebrated their triumph, savoring the shared joy and the knowledge that they were destined for greatness together.

As Alice and Sherlock reveled in their triumph, a hush fell over the studio. Emily, the show's host, approached them with a mischievous smile. "Congratulations on conquering the challenge," she said. "But remember, the path of love is never without hurdles."

Alice and Sherlock exchanged puzzled glances, their curiosity piqued. Emily continued, "In the next phase of the show, you will face a series of emotional tests that will challenge your commitment to each other. It's not just about conquering physical obstacles; it's about navigating the complexities of love."

A mixture of excitement and apprehension filled the air. Alice and Sherlock could feel the weight of the upcoming challenge, knowing that it would require them to confront their deepest emotions and vulnerabilities. Their connection would be put to the test once again, and they had to be prepared to face whatever lay ahead.

With a knowing smile, Emily left them with a parting remark. "Remember, love is a journey filled with ups and downs. It's how you navigate the obstacles that truly matters."

Alice and Sherlock looked at each other, their eyes filled with determination. They knew that their relationship would be tested like never before, but their hearts were resolute. They were ready to face the challenges that awaited them, their commitment to each other unyielding.

As the chapter drew to a close, the reader was left with a sense of anticipation. How would Alice and Sherlock navigate the emotional tests that awaited them? Would their bond withstand the trials that lay ahead? Only time would tell, and the reader eagerly awaited the next chapter, eager to witness the evolution of their relationship in the face of new obstacles.

CHAPTER 8: CONFRONTATION & ACCEPTANCE

Alice and Sherlock found themselves in a quiet corner of the studio, basking in the afterglow of their recent triumph. The air around them crackled with a potent mix of emotions — excitement, relief, and a tinge of uncertainty. They had come a long way since their first meeting, but they knew that their journey was far from over.

As they gazed into each other's eyes, a silent understanding passed between them. They were about to enter the next phase of the show, where the challenges would become even more intense, pushing their limits and testing their connection in ways they couldn't yet comprehend. The anticipation weighed heavy on their hearts, mingled with a sense of unease.

Alice's hand reached out, intertwining her fingers with Sherlock's, seeking comfort and reassurance. They drew strength from each other, their bond solidified through shared triumphs and moments of vulnerability. But deep down, they couldn't help but wonder what lay ahead. Would their newfound connection withstand the challenges they were about to face? Could their love endure the pressure of the show's relentless demands?

In the midst of their reflections, Emily, the show's host, approached them with a smile, breaking the solemnity of the moment. She sensed the mixed emotions swirling in the air and offered a few words of encouragement, reminding them of their resilience and the extraordinary journey they had embarked upon.

As Alice and Sherlock prepared to face the unknown, they held onto the belief that their love was worth fighting for. They were determined to confront whatever obstacles lay ahead, together. With a renewed sense of purpose and a shared commitment to their relationship, they took a deep breath, ready to take on the next phase of the show and whatever challenges awaited them.

The emotional tests they faced were unlike anything Alice and Sherlock had experienced before. As they delved deeper into the challenges, hidden insecurities and unresolved issues began to surface, casting a shadow over their relationship. The once harmonious connection now faced unsettling tensions that threatened to strain their bond.

Alice found herself grappling with feelings of vulnerability and self-doubt. The weight of her past experiences and the fear of repeating past mistakes loomed large in her mind. She questioned whether she was truly deserving of love and whether she could fully let go of her emotional baggage. These doubts began to color her interactions with Sherlock, creating a barrier between them.

Sherlock, too, faced his own internal struggles. His analytical mind analyzed every interaction, searching for signs of weakness or potential pitfalls. The fear of being hurt again, of allowing someone too close, made him cautious and guarded. This guardedness created a barrier of its own, preventing him from fully opening up to Alice and expressing his deepest emotions.

As the tensions grew, communication became strained. Honest conversations became more difficult as both Alice and Sherlock grappled with their own insecurities. Misunderstandings arose, and their once effortless connection now required intentional effort to bridge the growing gap.

Yet, amidst the challenges, Alice and Sherlock recognized the importance of open communication and vulnerability. They knew that they had to confront these issues head-on if they wanted their relationship to endure. With courage, they began to share their fears, their insecurities, and their hopes for the future.

It was not an easy process. There were tears, moments of frustration, and uncomfortable conversations. But with each difficult discussion, a sense of clarity emerged. They discovered that by acknowledging and addressing their individual struggles, they could find common ground and support each other through the healing process.

Slowly but surely, the tensions began to dissipate. As they navigated the emotional tests together, they realized that their bond was stronger than the challenges they faced. Their commitment to open and honest communication laid the foundation for deeper understanding and empathy.

Through acceptance and understanding, Alice and Sherlock discovered that their vulnerabilities and insecurities were not obstacles to their relationship, but opportunities for growth. The emotional tests became catalysts for their personal development and the strengthening of their connection.

As they emerged from this chapter of confrontation and acceptance, they were filled with a renewed sense of purpose and a deeper appreciation for the resilience of their love. They were ready to face whatever lay ahead, armed with the knowledge that true intimacy requires vulnerability, honesty, and a commitment to growth.

In the midst of their turmoil, Alice and Sherlock recognized the need for honest and heartfelt conversations. They sat down, facing each other, ready to confront the underlying conflicts and fears that had surfaced. It was a moment of vulnerability, as they bared their souls and exposed their deepest wounds.

Alice spoke first, her voice filled with raw emotion. She shared her fears of being hurt again, the scars left by past relationships that still haunted her. She acknowledged the walls she had built around her heart, shielding herself from the possibility of pain. As tears streamed down her face, she expressed her desire for a love that could break down those barriers and help her heal.

Sherlock listened attentively, his eyes filled with compassion. He understood her pain, having experienced his own share of heartbreak. He opened up about his own fears, his reluctance to fully commit out of fear of losing someone again. He admitted to the struggles of vulnerability and the challenge of letting someone see the depths of his emotions.

Their heartfelt conversations allowed them to see each other's wounds and acknowledge the barriers that stood in the way of their love. With every word spoken, they fostered a deeper understanding of each other's pain and hopes for the future.

Through their shared vulnerability, they began to find common ground. They reassured one another that their love was worth the risks and that they were both committed to working through their individual struggles. They offered support and acceptance, promising to be patient as they unraveled the layers of their wounded hearts.

In these heartfelt conversations, Alice and Sherlock discovered a profound sense of connection. They realized that their struggles and insecurities were not weaknesses but a part of their shared humanity. By confronting their fears head-on and embracing their vulnerabilities, they found a renewed strength within themselves and within their relationship.

As they continued to delve into their deepest emotions, they learned to extend grace and understanding to one another. They recognized that healing and growth would take time, but they were willing to embark on this journey together. With every conversation, they deepened their bond, building a foundation of trust and acceptance.

Through these heartfelt conversations, Alice and Sherlock found solace in each other's arms. They discovered that by facing their conflicts and fears head-on, they could pave the way for a love that was stronger and more resilient. Their commitment to open and honest communication became the guiding light on their path to healing and a deeper connection.

As Alice and Sherlock delved deeper into their heartfelt conversations, they realized that they had reached a crucial turning point in their relationship. The emotional breakthroughs they experienced were profound and transformative, allowing them to shed the weight of their past baggage and embrace a path of healing and growth.

In the safety of each other's presence, they fully expressed their feelings, allowing their vulnerability to become their greatest strength. Walls crumbled, and masks fell away as they confronted their fears head-on. It was not an easy process, as old wounds were reopened and emotions ran high. But in their shared journey, they found solace and understanding.

Alice spoke from the depths of her heart, releasing the pain that had plagued her for so long. She let go of the insecurities that held her back, acknowledging that she deserved love and happiness. With each word, she felt a weight lifting off her shoulders, and a newfound sense of freedom enveloped her.

Sherlock, too, opened himself up in ways he never thought possible. He confronted the deep-rooted fears that had kept him guarded, allowing himself to be vulnerable with Alice. As he let go of his past hurts and embraced the present moment, he felt a sense of liberation and a growing confidence in their connection.

Together, they created a safe space for honesty and acceptance. They held each other's hands, offering comfort and reassurance as they embarked on this emotional journey. They discovered that in sharing their vulnerabilities, they were not weakened but strengthened.

As their emotional breakthroughs unfolded, Alice and Sherlock witnessed a profound transformation within themselves and their relationship. The walls that once separated them had crumbled, replaced by a deep understanding and empathy for one another. They became each other's pillars of support, ready to face the challenges ahead with resilience and determination.

With every emotional layer they shed, their connection deepened. They realized that their shared vulnerability was the catalyst for a love that was not only passionate but also enduring. It was a love that celebrated both their strengths and imperfections, fostering growth and acceptance.

In embracing their emotional breakthroughs, Alice and Sherlock discovered the power of letting go and opening their hearts to the possibility of a brighter future together. They knew that healing and growth would be an ongoing process, but they were committed to taking the necessary steps, hand in hand.

With newfound clarity and a stronger bond, Alice and Sherlock embarked on the next chapter of their journey, ready to face the challenges and joys that lay ahead. Their emotional breakthroughs had paved the way for a love that was resilient, authentic, and capable of withstanding any obstacles that came their way.

As Alice and Sherlock stood at the crossroads of their relationship, they were faced with difficult choices that would shape their future together. The weight of their past hurts and the lingering scars of their individual journeys lingered in the air, presenting a formidable challenge to the love they had cultivated.

In the midst of uncertainty, they knew that they couldn't move forward without addressing the question that hung between them: Were they willing to let go of their past hurts and fully embrace the possibilities of love? It was a question that demanded introspection, vulnerability, and a willingness to confront their deepest fears.

Alice, drawing upon her newfound strength, reflected on the transformative power of love. She realized that holding onto past hurts would only hinder their ability to build a future together. With conviction in her voice, she vowed to let go of the pain that had held her captive, choosing instead to embrace the love that bloomed between her and Sherlock.

Sherlock, known for his analytical mind, wrestled with the implications of his choices. He understood the risks involved in opening his heart fully, but he also recognized the immense rewards that awaited him. With a mix of trepidation and determination, he decided to take a leap of faith, willing to confront his own vulnerabilities and embrace the love that had captivated him.

Their choices were not made lightly, for they understood the weight and consequence of their decisions. They knew that navigating the path of love required courage, resilience, and unwavering commitment. The journey ahead would demand their utmost vulnerability and a willingness to confront the shadows of their past.

As Alice and Sherlock made their choices, a renewed sense of purpose filled the air. They were determined to create a future built on trust, understanding, and shared growth. They recognized that their love was worth the risks, the sacrifices, and the effort required to heal and build something beautiful together.

In embracing the possibilities of love, Alice and Sherlock found solace in knowing that they were not alone in their journey. They had each other, and they had the unwavering support of a love that defied the odds. They were ready to face the challenges that lay ahead, armed with the knowledge that their commitment and determination would guide them through any storm.

With hearts intertwined and a shared vision of the future, Alice and Sherlock set forth on a path that promised growth, passion, and a love that would transcend the trials of life. Their choices marked a turning point in their journey, a testament to their unwavering belief in the power of love and their unwavering commitment to each other.

As they embraced the possibilities before them, they understood that the road ahead would not always be smooth. But with their hearts open and their spirits united, they were ready to face the unknown, knowing that together, they could conquer anything that came their way.

With renewed determination and a shared commitment to love, Alice and Sherlock embarked on the next chapter of their extraordinary journey, their hearts filled with hope, anticipation, and the unwavering belief that their love was destined to flourish. As Alice and Sherlock stood at the precipice of their relationship, they knew that the choices they made would shape their future. With hearts intertwined and a deepening love, they reaffirmed their commitment to each other.

In the midst of challenges and uncertainties, Alice and Sherlock recognized the strength of their bond. They acknowledged the obstacles they had already overcome, the barriers they had dismantled, and the wounds they had begun to heal. Each hurdle they faced had only strengthened their connection, reminding them of the depth of their love and the resilience within their hearts.

With vulnerability and honesty, they expressed their desires for a shared future—a future built on trust, understanding, and acceptance. They recognized that their journey would not be without its challenges, but they were willing to face them together, hand in hand.

Alice spoke from the depths of her heart, her voice filled with unwavering conviction. She expressed her love for Sherlock, acknowledging the growth they had experienced as individuals and as a couple. She shared her dreams of a life filled with adventure, laughter, and unwavering support. Her words echoed with sincerity, leaving no doubt about her commitment to their shared journey.

Sherlock, known for his analytical mind and guarded heart, opened himself up in ways he had never imagined. He bared his soul, expressing his love for Alice with a vulnerability that surprised even himself. He spoke of their shared experiences, the transformative power of their connection, and his unwavering belief in their ability to overcome any obstacle that lay ahead.

As their words intertwined and their hearts synchronized, Alice and Sherlock made a pact to build a future grounded in trust and mutual understanding. They vowed to cherish each other's individuality, to celebrate their shared moments, and to navigate the complexities of life with grace and resilience.

With their love as their guiding compass, Alice and Sherlock embarked on a journey filled with limitless possibilities. They understood that challenges would arise, and doubts might occasionally creep in, but they were determined to face them head-on, armed with a love that could weather any storm.

As they looked towards the horizon, their hearts brimming with hope and anticipation, Alice and Sherlock knew that their journey together would be nothing short of extraordinary. They had overcome the hurdles of the past, and now they stood ready to embrace the future, hand in hand, united in their unwavering love and commitment to each other.

Alice and Sherlock emerged from the depths of their confrontation with a renewed sense of clarity and purpose. The weight of unresolved conflicts had been lifted, replaced by a profound understanding and acceptance of each other. They had chosen to leave behind the shadows of the past, embracing a fresh start and a future filled with love and growth.

Hand in hand, they set intentions for their relationship, outlining the steps they would take to nurture their connection. They vowed to prioritize open and honest communication, never allowing their fears or insecurities to fester in silence. They committed to actively listening to each other, creating a safe space for vulnerability and understanding.

Alice and Sherlock recognized the importance of nurturing their individual growth alongside their shared journey. They encouraged each other to pursue their passions, supporting dreams and aspirations that extended beyond their relationship. They understood that personal growth would only strengthen the foundation of their love.

Together, they envisioned a life filled with adventure, laughter, and unwavering support. They spoke of their desire to create a home where love thrived, a sanctuary where they could find solace in each other's arms. They promised to cherish the small moments, to celebrate milestones, and to cultivate a love that would withstand the tests of time.

As they gazed into the future, Alice and Sherlock felt a profound sense of hope and excitement. They understood that their journey would not be without its challenges, but they were prepared to face them together. With hearts aligned and souls entwined, they embarked on a path illuminated by the light of their love.

Alice and Sherlock embraced the uncertainty of the future, knowing that their commitment to each other would guide them through the storms and the calm seas. They vowed to remain steadfast in their love, to support and uplift one another as they traversed the unknown.

Their hearts brimming with hope and determination, Alice and Sherlock stepped into the next chapter of their story. They carried with them the lessons learned, the growth achieved, and the unwavering love that bound them together. With every step they took, they knew that their journey would be nothing short of extraordinary, and they were ready to embrace the adventure that awaited them.

As Alice and Sherlock reveled in their newfound clarity and commitment, unaware of the storm brewing on the horizon, a sudden twist in the show's format cast a shadow over their blossoming love. The final moments of the chapter revealed a new challenge, one that would put their relationship to the ultimate test.

The air crackled with tension as the host, Emily, unveiled the unexpected twist that awaited Alice and Sherlock. Their bond would be tested in ways they could never have imagined, pushing them to their emotional limits and forcing them to confront the depths of their love.

A sense of unease settled upon Alice and Sherlock, their gazes meeting with a mix of determination and trepidation. They had come so far, overcoming numerous obstacles and conquering their own fears, but this new challenge threatened to unravel everything they had built.

Questions swirled in their minds. Could their love withstand this new trial? Were they truly prepared for what lay ahead? Doubts and insecurities resurfaced, but they refused to let fear overshadow their commitment.

Alice and Sherlock locked eyes, their silent vow echoing between them. They would face this challenge head-on, united in their determination to protect the love they had fought so hard to cultivate. They knew the road ahead would be arduous, filled with unexpected twists and turns, but their connection ran deep, anchoring them in the face of uncertainty.

As the chapter drew to a close, the reader was left on the edge of anticipation, yearning to discover how Alice and Sherlock would navigate the challenges that awaited them. Would their love prove resilient, or would they succumb to the trials that lay ahead? The answer remained shrouded in mystery, leaving the reader hungry for the next chapter, eager to witness the strength of their bond and the depth of their love in the face of the ultimate test.

CHAPTER 9: FINALE

Alice and Sherlock stood side by side, their hands tightly clasped, as they gazed out at the grand stage before them. The vibrant lights illuminated the set, casting an ethereal glow on their faces. The echoes of their footsteps mingled with the buzz of excitement that filled the air. It was the finale, the culmination of their journey on the show.

As they took a moment to reflect, memories of their shared experiences flooded their minds. They remembered the first time their paths crossed, the immediate connection that sparked between them. They recalled the challenges they had faced together, the obstacles that had tested their resilience and commitment. Each trial had only served to strengthen the bond they had forged.

Alice's heart swelled with gratitude as she thought about how far they had come. This journey had transformed her life, reigniting her passion for adventure and opening her heart to love once again. Sherlock, ever the enigmatic figure, had unraveled the mysteries of her soul, showing her a world beyond the pages of the books she adored.

Sherlock, too, marveled at the path they had traveled. He had never expected to find a love as profound as this, one that would not only challenge his intellect but also nourish his soul. Alice had breathed life into his existence, reminding him of the joy and wonder that could be found in even the simplest moments.

As they stood there, their eyes locked, they silently acknowledged the love that had blossomed between them. It was a love built on shared experiences, deep conversations, and the unwavering support they had shown each other. They were ready to face the final challenge, knowing that their connection would guide them through whatever lay ahead.

With a renewed sense of determination, Alice and Sherlock took a deep breath, ready to embrace the last hurdle. Their hearts beat in sync, fueled by the love they had found in each other. They stepped forward, ready to conquer the final challenge and emerge as victors not only in the show but in their own hearts.

The stage was set, and the spotlight awaited them. The finale beckoned, promising a culmination of their journey and a future that held endless possibilities. With nerves tinged with excitement, Alice and Sherlock stepped into the unknown, ready to show the world the power of their love.

Emily, the host of the show, stood at the center of the stage, her voice resonating through the venue. The crowd hushed in anticipation, waiting to learn the details of the final challenge. Alice and Sherlock exchanged a glance, their hearts pounding in unison.

With a mischievous smile, Emily revealed the ultimate test that awaited them. It was a combination of physical and emotional trials, carefully designed to push them to their limits. The challenge demanded not only strength and agility but also a deep understanding of each other's fears and vulnerabilities.

As the specifics were unveiled, Alice and Sherlock felt a surge of excitement mingled with a tinge of apprehension. The obstacles they would face were daunting, requiring them to confront their deepest fears and insecurities. They knew it would be a true testament to the growth they had experienced together.

Alice's voice trembled slightly as she turned to Sherlock, her eyes reflecting a mix of determination and vulnerability. "We've come so far, Sherlock. This challenge is the culmination of everything we've learned and overcome. We need to trust in ourselves and in each other."

Sherlock nodded, his gaze unwavering as he placed a hand on Alice's shoulder. "You're right, Alice. We've faced countless challenges together, and each one has made us stronger. We can do this. We have the strength and the bond to conquer whatever comes our way."

With a renewed sense of purpose, Alice and Sherlock embraced the final challenge. They faced each trial with unwavering commitment, pushing past physical exhaustion and emotional barriers. They leaned on each other for support, offering words of encouragement and a steady presence in the face of adversity.

Throughout the challenge, their connection deepened even further. They relied on their shared experiences, their unspoken understanding, and their unbreakable trust. Together, they overcame the obstacles that lay in their path, their resilience shining through with every step.

As they reached the final stage, their bodies weary but their spirits aflame, Alice and Sherlock locked eyes, a silent affirmation passing between them. They had grown individually and as a couple, conquering their fears and emerging stronger than ever.

The crowd erupted in applause as Alice and Sherlock stood at the pinnacle of the challenge. They had showcased their growth, their unwavering commitment, and the power of their bond. In that moment, they realized that their journey on the show had transformed into something much more profound—a love that would endure beyond the confines of the television screen.

As the applause faded, Alice and Sherlock stood hand in hand, their hearts intertwined. They had passed the final test, proving that their connection was unbreakable. The stage was now set for the next chapter of their lives, filled with infinite possibilities and a love that had been tested and proven true.

With gratitude in their hearts, Alice and Sherlock basked in the joy of their triumph. They knew that their journey was far from over, but with each challenge they had faced together, their love had grown stronger. They were ready to embrace the future, hand in hand, as they stepped off the stage and into a new chapter of their lives.

Each step of the final challenge presented Alice and Sherlock with new hurdles to overcome. They faced their fears head-on, pushing through physical exhaustion and mental fatigue. Doubts would creep in at times, threatening to undermine their confidence, but they refused to let them consume their spirits.

In the midst of the trials, Alice and Sherlock found solace in each other's presence. They drew strength from their unwavering support and unwavering belief in one another. When one stumbled, the other was there to lend a helping hand and a word of encouragement, reigniting the fire within.

There were moments of breathtaking triumph, where they conquered obstacles that seemed insurmountable. The joy and relief that washed over them were accompanied by a renewed sense of purpose. They could see the finish line, the culmination of their journey, just within reach.

But there were also moments of doubt and uncertainty, when the weight of the competition threatened to cloud their vision. They questioned whether they were deserving of victory, whether their love was strong enough to withstand the pressures of the outside world. In those moments, they leaned on each other, reminding themselves of the journey they had traveled together and the growth they had achieved.

With every challenge they conquered, their bond deepened, fortified by the shared experiences and the trials they had faced side by side. They discovered the true strength of their connection, the resilience that came from embracing vulnerability and pushing beyond their comfort zones.

As they neared the final moments of the challenge, Alice and Sherlock locked eyes, their hearts beating in unison. They had given their all, pushing themselves to the limits, and now it was time to release their grip on the outcome. The result would not define their love or the depth of their connection.

Hand in hand, they crossed the finish line, the weight of the challenge finally lifting from their shoulders. In that moment, they knew they had won something far more valuable than a competition—they had won the assurance of their love and the knowledge that they were capable of overcoming any obstacle together.

As the applause of the crowd filled the air, Alice and Sherlock shared a tender embrace, their hearts overflowing with gratitude and pride. They had emerged victorious, not just in the show, but in their journey of love and self-discovery.

The final challenge had tested them in ways they never could have anticipated, but it had also forged a bond that was unbreakable. They stood together, ready to face whatever lay ahead, knowing that their love was their greatest strength and that they were destined for a future filled with endless possibilities.

With each challenge, Alice and Sherlock held onto their love as an anchor, grounding them in moments of uncertainty and doubt. It served as a constant reminder of why they embarked on this journey in the first place—to find a love that transcends the confines of reality TV.

In the face of adversity, their love only grew stronger. It fueled their determination to persevere, pushing them to new heights and inspiring acts of courage they never thought possible. They found solace in each other's arms, drawing strength from the unwavering support and belief they shared.

When the world around them seemed chaotic and unpredictable, Alice and Sherlock created their own sanctuary within their love. It became a haven where they could find peace, understanding, and unwavering acceptance. In each other's embrace, they found the courage to face their fears and confront the challenges head-on.

Their love became the compass that guided them through the ups and downs of the show. It reminded them of their shared purpose and the unwavering commitment they had made to each other. They knew that no matter the outcome, their love would endure.

As they faced the final moments of the show, Alice and Sherlock held onto their love with a fierce determination. They knew that the true victory lay not in winning the competition, but in the depth of their connection. They had already won the most important prize—the love they had found in each other.

In the end, Alice and Sherlock emerged as victors, not just in the show but in love. Their journey had tested their limits, but it had also revealed the depth of their love and the strength of their bond. They had overcome the odds, proving that love can triumph over any challenge.

As they walked off the set, hand in hand, their hearts filled with joy and a renewed sense of purpose. They were ready to embark on the next chapter of their lives, knowing that their love would continue to be their guiding light.

The finale marked not just the end of a competition, but the beginning of a beautiful love story. Alice and Sherlock knew that their love was the foundation upon which they would build their future. With their hearts intertwined, they were ready to face whatever challenges lay ahead, knowing that together, they could conquer anything.

And as they walked into the sunset, their love shining brightly, the world watched in awe and admiration. Alice and Sherlock's love story had captured the hearts of millions, inspiring others to believe in the power of love and the possibility of finding their own happily ever after.

As the final challenge reached its climax, Alice and Sherlock stood at a crossroads, their hearts heavy with the weight of the decision before them. The grand prize shimmered tantalizingly in front of them, promising wealth, fame, and recognition. But as they locked eyes, a profound realization washed over them both.

In that moment, they knew that their love was worth more than any prize the show could offer. It was a love that had weathered storms, overcome obstacles, and grown stronger with each passing day. It was a love that transcended the confines of a reality TV competition, reaching into the depths of their souls.

With resolute determination, Alice and Sherlock made their choice. They turned their backs on the grand prize, leaving behind the allure of material gain. Instead, they chose to embrace the true treasure they had discovered—each other.

In the face of the show's host, the judges, and the millions of viewers watching, they declared their love for one another. Their decision reverberated through the studio, leaving an indelible mark on the hearts of all who witnessed it.

They knew that their love was a rare and precious gift, one that deserved to be cherished and nurtured above all else. The grand prize may have held temporary allure, but their love promised a lifetime of happiness and fulfillment.

As they walked away from the show's set, hand in hand, Alice and Sherlock felt a profound sense of liberation. They had chosen love over the trappings of success, and in doing so, they had gained something far more valuable—a future filled with love, passion, and unwavering devotion.

Their decision touched the hearts of millions, inspiring others to prioritize love and to recognize its immeasurable worth. Alice and Sherlock became symbols of courage and authenticity, reminding the world that love is the ultimate prize.

And so, they embarked on a new chapter of their lives—a chapter defined by the power of their love and the infinite possibilities that lay ahead. Together, they faced the future with open hearts, ready to conquer any challenges that came their way.

Their love story became a legend, whispered in the hearts of dreamers and romantics, a testament to the transformative power of love. And as they walked into the sunset, the world rejoiced, knowing that Alice and Sherlock had found a love that would withstand the tests of time.

The finale was not just the end of a TV show, but the beginning of an extraordinary love story. Alice and Sherlock had chosen love, and in doing so, they had discovered a happiness that surpassed all their expectations. Their love would forever be their greatest prize, cherished and celebrated, a beacon of hope for all who believed in the magic of love.

With unwavering resolve, Alice and Sherlock made their decision, choosing the path less traveled but filled with the promise of love and happiness. They stepped away from the grand stage of the show, leaving behind the glitz and glamour, and ventured into the uncharted territory of their own love story.

As they walked hand in hand, they knew that their journey had just begun. The cameras may have stopped rolling, but their hearts continued to beat with the rhythm of their shared dreams and aspirations. Together, they would navigate the challenges and joys that lay ahead, creating their own narrative, free from the constraints of a scripted reality.

The world watched in awe as Alice and Sherlock forged their own destiny, defying expectations and embracing the power of love. Their story became an inspiration to countless others, a reminder that true happiness lies in following the call of the heart, even when it means stepping away from the spotlight.

They faced the unknown with courage, trusting in the strength of their connection. Alice and Sherlock knew that their love was a force to be reckoned with, capable of withstanding any adversity that came their way. They were determined to build a life together, one filled with laughter, passion, and unwavering support.

In the days and months that followed, Alice and Sherlock celebrated each milestone, big and small, cherishing the moments of shared joy and overcoming the obstacles that life presented them. They nurtured their love, fostering a deep understanding and an unbreakable bond that grew stronger with every passing day.

Their story became a legend, whispered in the hearts of those who believed in the transformative power of love. Alice and Sherlock became beacons of hope, proof that taking a leap of faith in the name of love can lead to the most extraordinary adventures.

As they gazed into each other's eyes, Alice and Sherlock knew that they had made the right choice. Their decision to embrace their love had set them free, allowing them to discover a world of infinite possibilities together.

And so, they embarked on a new chapter, their hearts overflowing with gratitude and excitement. The finale was not the end, but a new beginning—a beginning that held the promise of a love story that would stand the test of time.

Alice and Sherlock's journey continued beyond the boundaries of the show, their love becoming the ultimate victory. They had found in each other the missing pieces of their souls, and together, they would create a love story that would inspire generations to come.

As they walked into the sunset, hand in hand, the world watched in awe, celebrating their triumph over adversity and their unwavering commitment to love. Alice and Sherlock had chosen love, and in doing so, they had discovered a happiness that surpassed all their wildest dreams.

Epilogue

Years had passed since Alice and Sherlock's journey on the show, and their love had blossomed into a beautiful tapestry woven with shared memories, laughter, and unwavering support. They had successfully blended their families, creating a harmonious home where love and acceptance thrived.

Their children had become not just step-siblings but confidants and companions, forming bonds that would last a lifetime. Together, Alice and Sherlock navigated the joys and challenges of raising their children, instilling in them the values of empathy, curiosity, and the power of love.

In their professional lives, Alice continued to inspire young minds as a literature teacher, while Sherlock's passion for criminology led him to become a renowned professor and consultant. They found fulfillment in their respective careers, supporting each other's ambitions and celebrating each milestone along the way.

The journey was not without its hurdles, as life often presented them with unexpected twists and turns. But through it all, Alice and Sherlock stood side by side, their love acting as a compass guiding them through the storms. They learned to communicate openly, to compromise, and to never lose sight of what truly mattered—their love and the happiness of their family.

Their love story had become an inspiration to others, with many seeking their guidance and wisdom. Alice and Sherlock graciously shared their experiences, encouraging others to embrace love, take risks, and create their own extraordinary stories.

As they sat together one evening, watching the sunset paint the sky with hues of gold and pink, Alice rested her head on Sherlock's shoulder. They exchanged a knowing glance, their eyes filled with a profound gratitude for the journey they had embarked upon.

"We've come a long way, haven't we?" Alice whispered, her voice filled with a sense of awe.

Sherlock smiled and gently squeezed her hand. "Indeed, my love. Our journey has been a testament to the power of love and the resilience of the human spirit. I am grateful every day for the love we share."

In that moment, they knew that their love had transcended the boundaries of time and space. It had become a force that not only enriched their own lives but touched the lives of those around them.

And as they embraced the future, hand in hand, Alice and Sherlock knew that their love story was far from over. It was a story that would continue to unfold, filled with new adventures, shared dreams, and a love that would withstand the tests of time.

The world watched in awe as Alice and Sherlock lived their happily ever after, knowing that true love, forged in the fires of adversity, could conquer all. Their love had become a beacon of hope, reminding everyone that love was not just a fairytale, but a real, tangible force that could transform lives.

And so, their love story continued, inspiring generations to come, and reminding us all that when we choose love, we choose a life of endless possibilities and infinite joy.

CHAPTER 10: EPILOGUE

Chapter 10: Epilogue

The sun cast a warm glow as Alice and Sherlock walked hand in hand along the beach, their footsteps leaving imprints in the sand. They had come a long way since their journey on the show, and their love had only grown stronger with time.

In the years that followed, Alice and Sherlock had built a life together filled with love, laughter, and shared adventures. They had faced the ups and downs of life with resilience and a deep commitment to each other.

Their relationship had become a true partnership, where they supported each other's dreams and aspirations. Alice had published her first novel, while Sherlock continued to make strides in his field, his expertise sought after by law enforcement agencies around the world.

Their blended family had flourished, their children thriving in an environment filled with love and understanding. The challenges of parenting were met with patience and open hearts, and their home was a sanctuary of warmth and acceptance.

As they walked along the beach, the waves gently lapping at their feet, Alice turned to Sherlock with a smile. "Do you remember when we first met on that reality show?"

Sherlock chuckled, his eyes sparkling with love. "How could I forget? It feels like a lifetime ago, and yet, it's as vivid as ever."

They shared a moment of quiet reflection, grateful for the journey that had brought them together. They had learned the true meaning of love, of resilience, and of embracing the beauty of the present moment.

Alice looked out at the horizon, her heart filled with hope and gratitude. "We've come so far, Sherlock. And I'm excited for what lies ahead."

Sherlock squeezed her hand, his voice filled with a mixture of pride and contentment. "As am I, Alice. Our love has withstood the tests of time, and I have no doubt that it will continue to blossom with each passing day."

They continued their walk, their steps in sync, their hearts intertwined. The world seemed to fade away as they reveled in the simple joy of being together.

The story of Alice and Sherlock had become a tale of resilience, of love that transcends all obstacles. Their journey had inspired others to take chances, to believe in the power of love, and to never give up on finding their own happily ever after.

And as the sun set, casting hues of pink and orange across the sky, Alice and Sherlock knew that their love story was not just an ending but a beginning—a beginning of a life filled with infinite possibilities, shared dreams, and a love that would endure for eternity.

In that moment, they knew that their love was the greatest adventure they would ever embark upon—a love that would continue to grow, evolve, and bring them joy, year after year.

Hand in hand, they walked into the sunset, ready to embrace the chapters that awaited them, knowing that their love was a story that would be cherished forever.

ABOUT THE AUTHOR

Emmanuel D. Simms Sr.

Emmanuel Simms is an American writer who is best known for his book The Rules of a Successful Failure. In his writing, he explores social issues such as race and discrimination within minority communities. Simms has a professional tone in his writing, which allows him to explore these difficult topics in a way that is both informative and relatable for his readers.

Simms grew up in a low-income, inner-city neighborhood. He witnessed firsthand the effects of discrimination and poverty on minority communities. This shaped his view of the world and inspired him to write about these issues in his books. In The Rules of a Successful Failure, Simms uses his personal experiences to explore what it takes to overcome adversity. He offers readers a unique perspective on the challenges faced by minorities in society and provides valuable advice on how to overcome them.

Simms' writing is important because it offers a rare look into the lives of minority communities. His insights can help readers to better understand the difficulties faced by these groups, and can provide hope to those who are struggling to overcome them.

BOOKS BY THIS AUTHOR

The Rules Of A Successful Failure: Paths Of A Local Icon (From The Creative Mind Of Emmanuel Simms Book 4)

Failure is one of the most common traits that anyone can have. It's so popular that striving for success is becoming as abstract as finding your true love before you turn twenty-seven. My story is simple. I haven't tried everything to reach my final goal yet, but for the things I have attempted to succeed I have only managed to fail. I am a successful failure. Use this book to your advantage as a guideline if you want to reach success these are the rules of a Successful Failure.

I Got It! Why Not Use It?: Gems I Had The Whole Time. (From The Creative Mind Of Emmanuel Simms Book 7)

This is a very special moment for me. Writing this book has been a therapeutic journey and I couldn't have done it without your support.
This book is designed to help people who are struggling with similar issues to what I have experienced. It's a guide to help you find your own strength and power within.
I believe that we all have the ability to heal ourselves. We just need to learn how to access that power. This book will show you how.
I am so grateful to have the opportunity to share this with all

of you. Thank you for your time and your support. I hope this book inspires you to make positive changes in your own life."This is a very special moment for me. Writing this book has been a therapeutic journey and I couldn't have done it without your support.

This book is designed to help people who are struggling with similar issues to what I have experienced. It's a guide to help you find your own strength and power within.

I believe that we all have the ability to heal ourselves. We just need to learn how to access that power. This book will show you how.

I am so grateful to have the opportunity to share this with all of you. Thank you for your time and your support. I hope this book inspires you to make positive changes in your own life

Mind 2 Mind: The Lost Book Of Poems And Psalms. (From The Creative Mind Of Emmanuel Simms 3)

Launchpad To Success: Make Your First $100K: Your Comprehensive Guide To Earning And Thriving

Embark on an empowering journey with "Launchpad to Success: Make Your First $100K". This book is your comprehensive guide to building a solid foundation for your entrepreneurial pursuits. It offers actionable insights, practical strategies, and real-world examples to help you navigate the challenges of entrepreneurship and achieve financial success. Whether you are a budding entrepreneur or a seasoned professional looking to take your career to new heights, this book provides you with the tools and knowledge you need to make your dreams a reality.

My Dad, Everywhere I Go (From The Creative Mind Of Emmanuel Simms Book 5)

Growing up, I remember always clinging to the men in my life in search of understanding who I was. My parents divorced when I was at a very young age, creating a lot of unsolved questions and disappointment. I wrote a poem when I was about eleven years old titled Come Home Daddy, and in 2013 I decided to make it into a children's book. This children's book is meant to advocate for the presence of black fathers in young black boy's lives. In the story, it talks about how I would see black men everywhere I go correlating them to being my dad. The story concludes how I see my dad everywhere except for home and my goal is to change that for other black boys like myself searching for answers only a father could give.

The Time We Spent

This story is about the last year I was blessed to get to know my dad. I seek to assist others through healing. The Time We Spent is for anyone who has or will take care of a parent. Times can get hard, but that's how we build our strength. I want to dedicate this book to all of the Great Hospice Workers out there, especially those who served my father with me during his last days.

My Feelings Family (From The Creative Mind Of Emmanuel Simms Book 2)

Join Gem as he introduces his family. There are many feelings, emotions, and faces that we experience daily this book seeks to assist our family to become more comfortable with their feelings. Have you ever felt or met any of these feelings before? Be sure to check in at the end with Gem when you reach the end.

Made in the USA
Middletown, DE
22 October 2023

40962104R00056